Shadow Lane Volume 3

The Romance of Discipline

by

Eve Howard

CCB Publishing
British Columbia, Canada

Shadow Lane Volume 3: The Romance of Discipline, Spanking, Sex, B&D and Anal Eroticism in a Small New England Village

ISBN-13 978-1-926585-29-1
Second Edition

Library and Archives Canada Cataloguing in Publication
Howard, Eve, 1953-
Shadow lane : volume 3: the romance of discipline, spanking, sex, b&d and anal eroticism in a small New England village / written by Eve Howard – 2nd ed.
ISBN 978-1-926585-29-1
Also available in electronic format.
I. Title.
PS3608.O82S533 2009 813'.6 C2009-903093-4

Cover artwork by Tarsis: www.briantarsis.com

Shadow Lane Volume 3 was originally published in episodic form in *Stand Corrected* magazine, Copyright © 1995 Eve Howard. Blue Moon first edition published 1995, Copyright © Eve Howard.

Publisher: CCB Publishing
British Columbia, Canada
www.ccbpublishing.com

This book is dedicated to every young lady who has ever had the courage to tell a man she's into spanking.

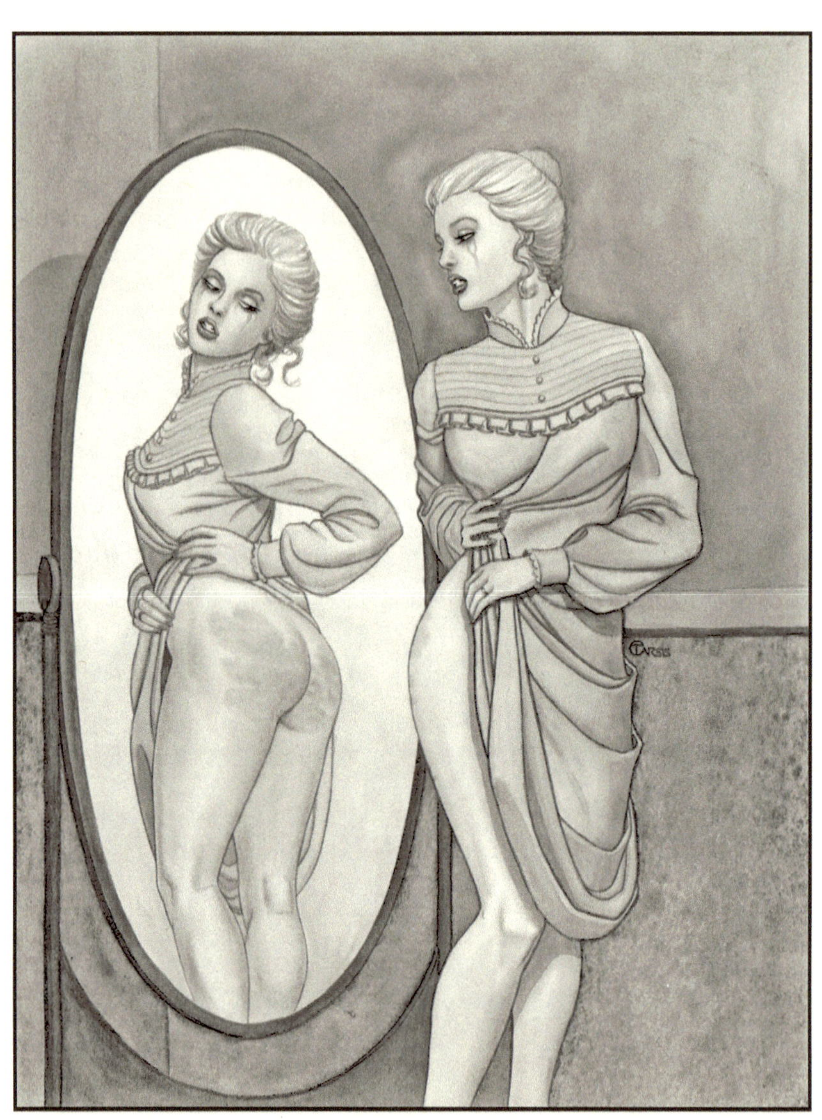

Shadow Lane

Volume 3

The Romance of Discipline,
Spanking, Sex, B&D and Anal Eroticism
in a Small New England Village

ꟃ

Contents

Chapter One

The Continuing Adventures of Susan Ross

At the beginning of October, Susan Ross sent her mentor, Hugo Sands, a written apology for her impertinence on the evening of Laura's caning the month before. A few days later, Hugo found himself in Manhattan and invited Susan to join him for a meal.

It was raining when the small blonde exited The Majestic Apartments on Central Park West to hail a taxi in the cool, damp, twilight air. The twenty year old wore her hair in a long ponytail and was dressed in a yellow oilcloth slicker and hat, pegged jeans and a white cotton shirt.

She was tense in the cab on the way across town. She had allowed her scene etiquette to lapse to the extent of defying Hugo, ruining a scene he'd been playing with her sister and breaking up a party at his own home. At the very least she expected him to be cross.

But Hugo surprised Susan by greeting her warmly. He removed her outer garments and brought her immediately to the most comfortable chair in his Doral Tuscany suite. He was a tall, lean, well-tailored man in his forties, with fair hair, pleasant features and an attractive demeanor, a fetish magazine publisher who had been a magnet for interesting submissive women for many years.

"Susan, I was touched by your letter," he told her fondly, "but please don't give that evening another thought."

"No?"

"Believe me, I'm not angry," he patted her pretty white hand. Susan looked at him in amazement.

"Then, I can come to your Halloween party?"

"Of course you can. Didn't Anthony receive an invitation yet?"

"I haven't seen Anthony since that night at your house," Susan admitted, flushing.

"Really?"

"I've been staying with Sherman Cooper."

"Susan, what's going on?" Hugo was shocked and alarmed.

"I daren't tell you."

"Why not?"

"You won't approve."

"Tell me anyway."

"You won't like it."

"Susan, I'm not renowned for my patience. Please explain."

"No offense, Hugo, but I wish Anthony would have stuck up for me more that night when you treated me like a 6 year old in front of everyone," Susan replied, with some trepidation.

"You were expecting chivalry and he behaved like a Roman," Hugo observed.

"Exactly!"

"Susan, don't you know that men are dogs?"

"Actually, I assumed that he refrained from interfering mainly out of courtesy to you, since you practically gave me to him in the first place, but whatever his motives were, his indifference disturbed me. You were being Basil Rathbone; he should have vanquished you."

Hugo smiled.

"Susan, you should get the paddling of your life for walking out on Anthony over this."

"I know. That's why I want to go to your party. I think it would be the best place to run into the Maestro and throw myself on his mercies."

"I wouldn't wait that long if I were you. I understand he's leaving for England in a couple of days and will be gone for most of the month. What's more, he's bringing a pretty new secretary over with him. And she's in the scene," Hugo fabricated blithely.

Susan's face drained of color and her heart began to pound.

"Boy, that was fast," she observed, feeling ill.

"Well, what did you expect? Aren't you at this very moment living with another man?"

"Yes, but it isn't like you think. Sherman isn't even in town," she explained.

Too distracted to remain any longer with Hugo, Susan wandered out into the night and again hailed a cab, anguished at the thought of Anthony's plane going down in the Atlantic before she had a chance to see him again.

It took a very long time to get down into the Village in the rush hour gridlock and Susan's eyes brimmed with tears more than once on the way.

Finally the taxi let her off at Anthony's red brick 3-story and she beheld with joy the silver Bentley parked at the curb. This meant that he was probably home and Susan rushed inside calling his name.

Anthony emerged at the top of the stairs, in the act of knotting a silk foulard tie and glanced at her with a coolness and reserve quite unlike him. She ran upstairs at once, tearing off her hat and slicker.

"Well?" he asked, folding his arms.

"I just came from Hugo. He said you were about to leave for England."

"He knows a lot more about my schedule than I do," Anthony replied.

"You're not going abroad?"

"No."

"Was Hugo also mistaken about your having a new secretary who's in the scene?"

"Would it bother you if I did?"

"I'd hate it."

"Funny, you haven't been acting that way," he observed, returning to the suite of rooms from which he had emerged. Susan followed and watched him pull on a double-breasted suit jacket of grey flannel.

"I'm sorry that I haven't," she exclaimed, "but do you have a new girlfriend or what?"

"I don't know. I suppose the girl I'm going out with tonight could become my girlfriend one day," he conjectured.

Susan paled at this painful supposition as her eyes blurred with tears.

"But I'm your girlfriend," she protested.

"No you're not."

Susan sunk onto a large, richly upholstered sofa and burst into sobs.

"Are you bringing her home with you tonight?" she dared to ask.

"What does it matter? You won't be here."

"Yes I will," she replied with spirit.

It was very difficult for Anthony to maintain an indifferent demeanor while his darling was in distress but he was hurt at being abandoned for five weeks. In addition, the fact that she had been living with his principal rival for her affections all month left him further incensed.

"In that case I won't come home."

"Please do!" she cried.

"No."

"Anthony, I can't believe that you don't love me anymore," Susan declared.

"The divine gift of my companionship has been squandered on you," he told her severely.

"That's not true! You know that you're my one and only," she quoted Gershwin, hoping to make him smile.

"Please, Susan, don't make me laugh."

"I mean in the greater scheme of things. Look, I'm just a kid. I don't understand the protocol of relationships yet."

"Is that so?" Anthony surveyed her guileless face with skepticism.

"The thing is, you're so busy and popular that I really thought you'd barely notice my absence."

"Susan, you're studying the wrong profession, you ought to be a lawyer," he told her, then added without humor, "now why don't you stop lying."

"All right, I hoped that if I disappeared for a while it would make you understand how disillusioned I was when you didn't protect me from Hugo Sands."

"What's this about Hugo Sands?" Anthony flashed back on the scene in Hugo's drawing room at the end of the summer and remembered with a start the look of mute appeal Susan had cast him after Hugo had ordered her to stand in the corner.

"You don't even remember the situation, do you?"

"Of course I remember. Hugo had a plan for the evening and you began to interfere, so he wound up turning you over his knee."

"In front of everyone."

"You wanted me to prevent him from doing that?"

"Yes!"

"And that's what your leaving me has been about?" Anthony was annoyed at himself for not having thought of this explanation before.

"Yes."

"I see."

"Oh, Anthony, I'm as sorry as can be about all of this."

"Oh? Why is that?"

"I'm sure you didn't mean to be callous. Now that I've spoken to Hugo I realize that you might have enjoyed being a Roman. After all, we're all in the scene and I was taking things too seriously, spoiling the fun. I guess I think too much."

He would have embraced her just then, but Anthony's sense of the theatrical demanded a postponement of their reconciliation.

"Well, I have a pressing engagement," he informed her, as though their conversation had begun to bore him.

"Couldn't you postpone it?"

"No."

"May I wait for you here?"

"No."

"I will anyway," she returned.

"You do and you'll get a good spanking. I'm about fed up with you."

Susan felt a terrible thrill at these words. Anthony dialed his driver Dennis on the in-house phone and told him to warm up the car. Immediately after he hung up, the phone rang again. Anthony picked it up and began to chat briefly with a friend. This small event gave Susan an idea and she ran upstairs.

Hardly knowing what motivated her, for she was not normally a madcap, Susan ran down the back stairs to the first floor, exited the building through the kitchen, slipped through the garden gate into the alley and then out to the street where Dennis had just gotten into the

Bentley. Susan made a dead run for the door, slipped into the passenger's side, front seat and startling the wits out of the young English driver, curled up on the floor under the dash, well out of sight.

"Miss Susan, what are you doing?"

"Don't give me away!" she commanded urgently.

Before Dennis, who had flushed deeply, could reply, Anthony opened the back door and got into the car. Susan tented her hands in a prayer to the driver.

"65th and Park, Dennis," said Anthony, settling back for the ride lost in thought.

Dennis, who adored Susan, was now in a quandary. He dared not risk offending his generous employer, but he couldn't think of betraying the young lady he most admired either. And yet why had she the need to play a prank like this? Deciding to ignore the situation and hope for the best, Dennis proceeded into the night.

"Dennis, it looks like Miss Susan is back with us," Anthony said casually from the back seat. Dennis gave a start as his employer continued, "So after you drop me off I want you to go back home and make yourself available to her in case she needs you."

"Very good, sir," said the chauffeur, enormously relieved. Dennis looked down and was horrified to read a note that Susan had scribbled for him to read.

"Get him to talk about me!" it read and Dennis visibly recoiled. But Susan persisted in pointing at the note until Dennis finally stammered, "I don't think Miss Susan likes to make use of the Bentley, Sir."

"Then put her in a cab if she wants to go out," Newton told him. "And make sure there's plenty of wood in her fireplace too."

Susan smiled, touched.

"I will, Mr. Newton."

Sixteen minutes later, Dennis pulled to a stop in front of the elegant old apartment building where Anthony was picking up his date.

"I'll find my own way home," said Anthony, getting out of the car. Dennis immediately pulled away from the curb. Susan waited until he'd gone a quarter block before scrambling up on the seat with cramped arms and legs.

"Go around the block and park just short of the building. I want to see them come out," Susan ordered.

"Must I, Miss Susan?"

"I asked you to, didn't I?"

"What if he sees us?"

"Make sure he doesn't."

Dennis circled the block and parked on the opposite side of the street. Then they waited.

"Perhaps he won't come out at all," said Dennis.

"It's dinner time. They have to come out to eat," Susan told him. And sure enough, within 5 minutes, Anthony emerged beneath the bottle green awning with a sleek brunette in her middle thirties. As the uniformed doorman hailed them a cab, Susan had ample time to absorb every detail of the slender beauty's skirt suit and overcoat ensemble. The hat, gloves, purse and spectator pumps were perfectly coordinated. White skin, black hair, red mouth, and patrician nose. Susan observed the gracefulness of her shoulders, neck and instep. The woman had a propensity to smile and laugh good-naturedly that lent additional appeal to her well-bred appearance. Everything about her was sophisticated. Susan shuddered at the thought that this paragon of confident femininity should also be inclined to play at B&D.

"She's beautiful, isn't she, Dennis?" Susan observed as Anthony handed her into a cab.

"Quite nice," the driver agreed.

"Have you dropped him off at her place before?"

"I don't feel I'm at liberty to reveal that information, Miss Susan," said Dennis firmly.

"I see," replied Susan coolly.

"Where to, Miss?"

"West 72nd Street and the park," Susan said, folding her arms and staring out the rain streaked window.

"I'm sorry, Miss Susan, but you've put me in a very awkward position," Dennis explained.

"Dennis, stop over dramatizing," Susan recommended.

Deeply shocked at this harsh accusation, he nevertheless marveled at her discernment.

"I think you're a conceited boy who's being difficult because his mistress doesn't pay enough attention to him," Susan added incisively. At this pronouncement Dennis flushed a frightful shade of red.

"I've taken Mr. Newton to that address once before," the twenty-four year old Londoner caved in to the forcefulness of his employer's twenty year old girlfriend.

"And did he ever bring her home with him?" Susan demanded.

"Not that I know of."

"Thank you, Dennis."

They did not exchange another word until after Susan came down from the Majestic apartments with her textbooks and a valise. As before, she climbed into the front seat beside him, a gesture he could not fail to note with a throbbing heart.

"Home, Miss Susan?"

"Yes, thank you, Dennis."

Susan observed the color come and go in the young man's smooth, clear face as she said these few words to him. Impulsively she touched his thigh.

"I didn't mean to hurt your feelings, Dennis."

"Don't give it another thought, Miss Susan," Dennis replied, and then added, with painful shyness, "I want to serve you better."

Susan rewarded Dennis with a smile, aware that she had just acquired her first slave.

Anthony Newton arrived home around midnight and discovered Susan asleep on the overstuffed sofa before his bedroom hearth. She was dressed in a luxurious slate blue silk-satin gown set with matching mules. Her long hair hung about her shoulders in wheat-blonde waves. She awoke with a start the moment his light step crossed the threshold.

"Still here, are you?" he sat next to her on the couch. She shrunk back but he seized her little wrists and drew her across his lap with the ease of arranging a dinner napkin. "I told you what would happen if I found you here tonight, you horrible girl!"

Placing one hand firmly on her waist, Anthony smoothed the dressing gown down over her round little bottom then drew back his free hand and brought it down resoundingly on one cheek, then the other, until he'd administered at least three dozen sound smacks to the seat of her robe. Susan bit her lip and did not argue, though she couldn't help but kick her little feet each time his hand came down.

"So you think that you can leave and come back whenever you like, do you?" he demanded, continuing to spank her harder still. Susan wriggled on his knees and tried to shield her bottom with her hand, the wrist of which he grabbed and pinned to the small of her back firmly before continuing. "No you don't," he told her, pulling the smooth layers of satin gown and robe up to her waist to reveal her already blushing bottom. After laying it bare he surveyed it for a long moment, holding her in place while she held her breath. But before striking her, he wound his hand in her hair and carefully but coolly made her look at him.

"You deserve to be punished, don't you?"

"Yes, sir," Susan replied in a voice that caused him to release her wheaten hair and pause to arrange her perfectly across his lap.

"You've treated me quite badly, and for no good reason," Anthony said.

"I deeply regret that," she cast an appealing look back at him.

It was becoming increasingly difficult for Anthony, with this adorable package of compliance prone across his knees, to remain even mildly disgruntled, no less angry.

"You're just a spoiled little girl," he told her, taking a firmer hold on her waist before applying his palm to her bottom for twelve to fifteen minutes. Holding her in place, Anthony spanked her with metronomic precision, never altering his rhythm and always bringing his hand down hard after skipping two beats in between smacks. Penetrating heat combined with an ever-increasing sting caused Susan to jerk and wriggle across her man's muscular thighs. Little whimpers began to escape her lips as the spanking continued, with the tempo increasing to one beat between smacks. Susan began to feel very sorry indeed for her behavior and felt the justness of the discipline. Anthony had never been anything other than charming and indulgent toward her, treating her like an adult and a friend although she was only a silly child not even through her undergraduate degree. Handsome, popular, even-tempered and enormously adept at seduction, Anthony had nevertheless reserved the first place in his heart for Susan and she had seemed to disregard the importance of this. Susan felt foolish now, as though she'd almost thrown away her most precious possession, the love of a truly exceptional man. Every slap struck a resounding cord in her tender soul as she luxuriated in the punishment that would expiate her error. Impressed by her silent acquiescence, Anthony paused and coolly forced her face up to examine it. She looked quite the fallen angel, with her full, trembling red lips and guilt-stricken blue eyes. Her soft, submissive posture and childish expression pierced his heart and electrified another important organ simultaneously. But now that she was absorbed with the drama of this midnight encounter he couldn't disappoint her by allowing the intensity to flag.

"Get up," he told her.

Susan slid off his lap and unconsciously rubbed her bottom through the satin gown and robe, sinking to her knees beside his chair.

"I said get up," he repeated, pulling her up. Susan blushed, feeling like a stupid child.

"That outfit is too sophisticated for you," he told her, as though the exquisite ensemble displeased him. "Go to your room and change into something more appropriate for a naughty little girl," he ordered.

Excited and upset, Susan went up to her studio. Anthony seemed quite angry with her. Of course she couldn't believe that deep down he was really angry with her. He was far too levelheaded to take the actions of a frivolous child like herself to heart. Susan felt a tiny thrill as she mused on her lover's age and experience. He was quite old enough to be her father, though he wore his 40 years very lightly. His importance in the real world endowed Anthony Newton with a natural dignity, which even an irreverent Ivy League brat like Susan was compelled to respect. It occurred to Susan that though he might never use the word himself, Anthony was her master. The coolness with which he had greeted her return this evening confirmed his control.

She knelt before her biggest marble topped chest, the one that contained her combinations and nighties and pulled out the bottom drawer, in which everything was of white cotton. She selected a waltz length eyelet trimmed gown and wrapper, which was laced with blue satin, ribbons and tied with a blue satin sash. In the set with her long, blonde hair down she might have sat for Renoir.

Anthony had removed his tie and jacket and was in the process of rolling up his sleeves when she returned to him. Rather than meeting his eyes, she scanned the counterpane which displayed a multi-thonged flogger, a razor strop and perhaps what frightened Susan the most, a long, broad, oval shaped wooden hairbrush.

"Come over here young lady," he ordered. "Give me your wrists." When she obeyed he tied them together in front of her with a pristine white handkerchief. They looked at each other.

"You have something to say?" he asked her gravely.

"Only that I'm sorry," she replied.

"Sorry that you overreacted to the Random Point incident?" Anthony pulled her by her bound wrists face down across his lap and took up the hairbrush, which terrified Susan.

"Yes, I overreacted," she replied. He laid the back of the brush against the curve of her buttocks, which was fairly well protected by two layers of eyelet-sewn cotton.

"I hate to have to do this, Susan, but I feel I have to get your attention this time," he explained, drawing back his arm to deliver the first smack. The blow of this big brush was solid, imparting a sharp, deeply penetrating pain, which caused her to cry out with shock and dismay as she jumped on his lap.

"No!" she wrenched her upper torso around and tried to break free.

"What do you think you're doing?" he pushed her back down. Then he slowly applied the hairbrush with equal severity an additional half dozen times, holding her firmly in place across his knees with one hand on her waist all the while.

In his attic apartment Dennis heard his little mistress' anguish as her desperate cries rang through the house. Half mad with empathy and excitement, Dennis paced. He didn't know what state was to be more devoutly coveted, that of being Susan's resolute master or worshipful submissive.

"You know you've got this coming," Anthony uttered, with implacable certainty, raising her dressing gown and nightie.

"No more with the brush, I beg you!" She twisted and turned on his lap. He examined her blushing bottom, which revealed the dark rose imprint of the brush on her flawless white skin. Tears ran down her face as she gave him one stricken look then hung her head and burst into sobs. "Mercy!" she whimpered, repeating the plea several times before breaking down completely.

Anthony lifted her from his lap, setting her on her feet. He first untied her wrists, giving her the handkerchief to wipe her eyes, then untied her satin sash and pulled the wrapper from her shoulders. She was charming in the sleeveless, fitted, white, embroidered gown.

"No more with the hairbrush," he pulled her down to sit on his lap, encircling her small waist with his arms.

"Thank you," she murmured.

"I'm still angry with you, though."

"Are you really?"

"When would you have deigned to come back if it weren't for Hugo's lie about my new secretary and the trip abroad?"

"I was planning to run into you at Hugo's Halloween party," she confessed.

"Not until then?" Now Anthony was genuinely perturbed. "You intended to keep your distance for two months to prove a point?"

"Tony, we've traded E-mail every single day since I've been at Central Park West," she referred to their daily computer bulletin board message exchanges via the modem. "If you wanted me to come back to the Village so badly why didn't you say so?" Susan jumped off his lap.

"I guess I was waiting to see how long it would take you to decide to return on your own." He got up and paced.

"That and you were so busy up on Park Avenue that you barely noticed I was gone," Susan suddenly accused.

"What do you mean, Park Avenue? Susan Ross, did you follow me tonight?"

"What if I did?" Susan challenged.

"Worse and worse!"

"Oh Anthony, I've missed you!" she tried to put her arms around him but he didn't allow this.

"So much that you could afford to wait to run into me at a party a month from now?" Anthony was so piqued at this revelation that he lifted her onto the high, lavishly dressed four-poster bed saying, "We've got to get some things straightened out here. Arms around the post." He assisted in arranging Susan's arms so that she hugged the carved wooden bedpost with her graceful back turned towards him. He gathered up the skirt of her gown and tucked it up between her arm and the bedpost, baring her pink bottom. He took up the multi-thonged whip with its broad, flat, leather lashes and placed his other hand in the small of her back.

"Run into me at a party, will you?" he administered the first stroke directly across the fleshiest portion of her bottom in a vigorous manner, which caused her to catch her breath and rock with the lash.

"You know, Susan, you'd bore me to death if you didn't have a life of your own, but let's not lose perspective here." He delivered the next stroke lower and harder. Susan gave a little sob of fear.

"Are you my girl or aren't you?"

"You said I wasn't before," she murmured.

"Don't tell me what I said," he administered a third lash, which seemed to cover her entire bottom and left a pink bouquet of whip marks in its wake. "Your manners are getting worse and worse, Susan." He punctuated this accusation with the firmest stroke so far, one that caused her to cry out in pain and fear, while appealing to him with tearful eyes.

"Don't look at me like that. I'm very displeased with you," he told her, drawing back his arm to administer the end of the whipping. The two final strokes were frighteningly severe to Susan, who immediately sank down on her knees, hid her face and wept.

"Let's get back to you following me tonight. You can't possibly think that was the proper thing to do?" He lifted her head and quite coolly wiped her face with his handkerchief.

Susan looked guilty. "I just wanted to see the lady."

"Really! Well, thanks to your eleventh hour histrionics I had a perfectly awful time. I couldn't concentrate on anything besides what I was going to do to you when I got home."

"I'm sorry." Susan sank down on the pillows, profoundly relieved that he'd cast the whip aside and charmed that she'd preoccupied him all night. Her tears subsided as he continued to make repairs to her damp face with the handkerchief. Forced to scrutinize her dear face he could not resist bestowing a kiss on her full, red mouth. As she yielded to him he drew her against his chest and kissed her hard, on her lips, throat and bosom, which he also gently squeezed through the fine, embroidered gown.

"Your punishment isn't over," he told her, repressing the rising tide of sentimentality which suddenly engulfed him as he caressed her. Her passivity in his arms was intoxicating.

"Please, Anthony, the brush and whip hurt so much. Couldn't the remainder of my lesson be ... less stringent?" Susan requested hesitantly.

Anthony didn't answer immediately but continued to hold her.

"Perhaps," he said, at length, "we should visit the examining room."

Susan immediately flushed.

"Or is that concept too humiliating?" he asked, making her look at him.

"No, Sir."

"Do you think you could benefit from that sort of discipline?"

"Yes."

As Anthony led Susan upstairs to the luxuriously appointed Victorian examining room on the third floor, she clung to his hand, ashamed of the ache she began to experience in anticipation of what would soon be done to her bottom.

Once the door was locked behind them Anthony adjusted the lighting to his taste and deposited Susan in a leather armchair opposite a grand mahogany desk, behind which he then sat, in a corner of the room designated as a consulting area.

On the wall to Susan's right hung Anthony's several Ivy League and conservatory diplomas, each signifying a different degree of academic and musical accomplishment. The wall behind his desk held a pair of wood trimmed glass cases filled with volumes of arcane medical lore, which he had purchased at an estate auction to lend authenticity to this examining room, which he had installed in his townhouse for their mutual enjoyment.

"Well, young lady," said Anthony, slipping on a pair of glasses and sternly consulting her file, "I didn't expect to see you back at our clinic so soon."

"It's been six months," she protested.

"Has it, indeed?" Anthony, who was gratified that the date of their last appointment in this room had fixed itself so firmly in her mind, nevertheless frowned at her.

"Yes, Sir."

Susan understood that they had become characters in a fantasy. Anthony even got out a chart.

"Now then, Miss Susan, when was the last time you engaged in sexual intercourse?" Anthony asked blandly.

"Uh...do I have to answer?"

Anthony slammed his pen down on the desk.

"My dear girl, as the Director of this clinic, I assure you that all you reveal will be held in the strictest confidence."

"I don't remember," Susan smiled. "It was ages ago."

"I wonder how that can be when you've been residing with Lawyer Cooper all month."

"He's been out of the country. I've been alone all month."

"Oh!" Anthony was happily surprised, this simple admission placing Susan's absence in a different perspective.

"So you've just been alone, behaving yourself all this time?"

"I have mid-terms coming up and I've had some very large 18th century novels to read," she replied. Anthony highly approved of his pet's delicate education but could not allow the conversation to become either general or literary at this point.

"That's very admirable but surely a young girl like you can't have gone this long without a lover." Anthony returned to the character of clinical therapist.

"Come to think of it, William made love to me last month."

"Really!" Anthony pretended to be shocked though he already knew of Susan's adventure with her brother-in-law William Random.

Susan blushed, then volunteered, "He taught me how to come with just a vibrator through my clothes. I don't even need to have sex or anal penetration."

"Susan, you will always need to have sex and anal penetration. I can't imagine what William was thinking of."

"Well, we did have sex. But it was from the vibrator that I climaxed."

"I'm making a note of that. Now, what other naughty things have you done lately?"

"I found my first slave," Susan coolly announced, pointing to the corner of the building where Anthony's driver had his quarters.

"Dennis?"

"Actually, he's only my slave in theory so far. I haven't put it to the test yet."

"I see," Anthony gave her a look that promised an almost immediate trip across his knee, causing Susan to realize she had said a presumptuous thing. For a moment neither of them spoke, then Anthony rose to his feet.

"So, at 20 years old you've decided that you need to own a slave. And you have the effrontery to select him from my household staff!"

Susan bowed her head in embarrassment, peeking at her pacing lover from under her lashes. He frowned at her, deciding what sort of lesson her impertinence merited.

"Your arrogance is becoming insupportable," he declared. Susan didn't dare meet his eyes now.

"So you think my driver is your property, do you?" Anthony asked. Susan opened her mouth to reply but he stopped her. "Perhaps I should ask Dennis to join us so we can clear this matter up."

"You wouldn't humiliate Dennis like that," Susan protested.

"I wouldn't dream of humiliating Dennis. I was merely going to ask him whether, if given the choice, he'd prefer to straighten out Miss Susan's shoe closet or fuck the living daylights out of her. We know what a slave's reply would be."

Susan was taken aback by the notion that she might indeed have been mistaken in the English boy's ardor, interpreting his lust as romantic thralldom. Yet she could not refrain from replying, almost haughtily, "Slaves are weak, especially when presented with a temptation as alluring as the one you just described. However, I know your character too well to believe that you would ever initiate so crude a litmus test."

Anthony was astonished at her adroit handling of his volatile suggestion and began to think there was nothing that could put this irritating girl out of countenance.

"You realize of course that I can't possibly keep Dennis on," he let drop coolly.

"But, why not?" Susan went cold with fear. If her frivolousness caused a good man to lose his job she wouldn't be able to live with herself.

"You can't expect me to pay an employee to make love to my girlfriend."

"But he hasn't been!"

"Regarding you as his mistress is just as unacceptable to me," Anthony continued.

"But he doesn't regard me as that. Quite honestly, I only felt I had him in my power, so to speak, for the first time today. So you see, he doesn't know about any of this. Therefore, you have no reason to dismiss him."

"What you've told me is reason enough. What do you think this is, some B&D bawdy house? Dennis is my employee, not your personal plaything. He's at your disposal to run errands, drive you around and guard you on the streets. Nothing more. Do you understand?"

"Yes sir."

"That's good, because if I hear or observe one more hint that Dennis is anything more to you than an employee I will dismiss him immediately."

"I understand."

"I'm very angry about this and you're going to have to be severely punished."

Susan hung her head though her heart was racing.

"Take off your gown," he ordered, opening several drawers in the oaken cabinetry lining one wall and removing a polished wooden box from one and an antique black medicine bag from another, pausing to check on Susan in one of the mirrors as he did so. She looked worried, which satisfied him. "I said remove your gown," he repeated sternly and she quickly slipped it over her head, fully revealing her petite, exquisitely formed body.

"Come here," he told her, seating himself on a graceful Directoire recamier, affording ample room to sit with a girl across his lap. He made Susan stand still before him as he took various objects from the medical bag and polished wooden case and spread them out on an inlaid mahogany drum table to his right. From the medicine bag he drew items such as a thermometer, Vaseline, suppositories and a pre-mixed douche. While from the box he extracted several polished wooden dildos and one small, solid wooden paddle.

"You see all this?" he asked. She nodded, feeling that familiar ache between her legs. "This is to assist your rehabilitation. Once you've been disciplined and trained by all of these devices, you'll remember, in spite of yourself that what you really like best is to be submissive."

With that he took Susan across his lap and after positioning her comfortably, examined her bare bottom thoroughly.

Susan didn't dare argue as he lubricated her and then inserted the thermometer into her bottom.

She gasped as this was done.

"Don't fuss," he warned her, slapping her thigh rather sharply. Susan laid still, her face burning with shame, feeling like a helpless little girl. One hand held her by the waist, the other rested on her bottom. She buried her face in her arms. Presently he removed the thermometer and informed her that she was running a bit of a fever. Perhaps some melted ice would help to bring it down.

He instructed her to bring him some ice from the small pantry adjunct to the examining room where he kept various supplies in a refrigerator. Susan found a small ice bucket inside it filled with spherical ice cubes. She brought this to him on a tray with the tongs which he had also requested and allowed him to take her back across his lap. But this time he placed a thick white towel across his trousered legs before arranging her for maximum access to her flawless bottom. Separating her buttocks firmly, he inserted a harmless glycerin suppository between her cheeks and well up into her bottom. She squirmed, sobbed and whimpered in extreme embarrassment. He held in front of her face the first wooden dildo he had selected for her edification. This was a polished teak rod, with rounded ends, one inch around and about 7" in length. Anointing the slim wooden shaft with lubricant, he spread her cheeks and inserted one end into her anus, and holding her firmly apart, he slowly pushed most of this object into her rectum. He then allowed her bottom to contract around it and commanded her to lie completely still, which she found very difficult to do in the frenzy of excitement to which this methodical insertion had driven her. Tormenting her with minute adjustments in the angle and depth of insertion, he finally seemed satisfied with its positioning and proceeded to enhance its effect upon his pretty young lady by spanking her smartly. She began to pinken immediately. He stopped and selected the second solid wooden dildo, this one somewhat thicker around, and showed it to her. Then, without disturbing the first, he gently spread her thighs and inserted the larger, manlier object into her highly lubricated sex. The ache became unbearable as this long, cool rod slid slowly up into her pussy until only an inch or so depended from that snug, curl fringed orifice. Now, thus lewdly filled, Susan whimpered in shame as he adjusted the objects that penetrated her so deeply and fussed about the two separate points of entry. Because Susan was so wet and growing more so by the moment, the larger dildo began to slip out every few seconds and had to be pushed firmly back into that soaking, pulsing glove.

Then he tried something different. Telling her to lie completely still, Anthony gently relieved her of the slim rod that had been lodged so deeply in her bottom and laid it aside. Then he pulled towards them the bucket of ice cubes she'd brought him. The dildo he'd placed in her vagina remained where it was.

Spreading her bottom open, he inserted one of the melting ice cube balls into it, then simply held and stroked her firmly as she gasped in shock.

"That's okay, you need cooling off," he informed her, dividing her cheeks again to pop another ice cube through her anal ring. Susan wriggled on his lap and ground against his thighs. He noticed this and slapped her hard. "Did I not tell you to lie still? If you dare to have an orgasm before I give you permission, I'll cane you. Do you understand?"

"I can't control that," she protested, forcing herself to lie still.

"I told you to lie still," he spanked her. "That doesn't mean clench your bottom. It means no motion."

Susan felt deeply humiliated when her extreme lubricity caused the dildo to slip out of her vagina. He did not replace it, but punished her with a half dozen very hard smacks on either cheek to demonstrate his disapproval.

"Why did I even bother to treat you like a grown-up?" he asked, again separating her buttocks to insert another ice cube inside her bottom. The sensation provided by the melting balls was indescribably erotic to Susan, who also enjoyed the restraint of being made to hold still.

The next thing he showed her, in front of her face, was the disposable enema, which was a basic pint of mineral water in an applicator tipped plastic bottle.

"You're getting this next. And after that, another one. I'm taking your bottom tonight and I want it to be perfect."

Susan heard these words of love with trembling and passion but had little faith in her own ability to postpone her orgasm much longer. Particularly when he held her apart for the nozzle of the enema bottle and began to squeeze the liquid into her bottom. This did not take long and once the entire amount had been infused, he sealed the operation with a 5" rubber retention plug, which he inserted to the hilt and held in place with the palm of his hand.

With her tummy now slightly full, she couldn't help but begin to squirm across his lap. He held her firmly in place by the waist and did not let her wriggle for long.

"I told you to be still," he scolded, spanking her across the plug and also on either cheek. "Just this once you're going to learn to obey," he warned her, continuing to alternate between spanking her luscious buttocks and spanking the plug ever deeper into her bottom. This was not an unduly severe spanking, but it was a deeply humiliating one.

"Oh stop!" she begged. "I'm going to come if you don't."

"I told you you weren't to." Several hard smacks followed. "All right, I'm going to withdraw this plug and allow you to visit the commode."

Susan had to make her mind a complete blank in order to avoid succumbing to an orgasm as he withdrew the retention plug. Then she was allowed to leave him for a time.

When Susan returned, Anthony had set up an enema bag on an IV stand on wheels and he had placed it to the side of the leather upholstered examining table. It appeared very full to Susan.

"Get up on the table, Susan. I want your head down, your knees apart and your bottom uppermost. Immediately."

Susan timidly obeyed the command to mount the table and assume the specified position.

"Legs apart as far as they'll go," he told her, separating her knees firmly. He also pressed down in the small of her back to increase the upward thrust of her well-rounded buttocks. Next, he re-lubricated her anus, very gently, mindful of the activity which had already visited this sensitive region as well as the rest of the night's agenda.

"As you know, I'm not naturally inclined to be this strict with you, Susan, but your willfulness must be corrected."

Adding the nicety of a rubber glove, Anthony used his middle finger to deeply probe her bottom in the process of lubricating it.

"I will be using a Bardex nozzle," he told her, showing her the curious apparatus with which he was about to fill her. "This is very warm water so prepare yourself."

Susan hung her head and held her breath as he began to insert the rather busy nozzle that had connected to it a deflated rubber ball. Once this operation had been completed and the entire nozzle had been buried, causing Susan to feel momentarily dizzy with the magnitude of her humiliation, Anthony began to inflate the rubber ball in her bottom.

"As you probably figured out, the inflated rubber ball just inside your bottom will assist you in retaining the enema you're about to receive."

Susan's face burned as she submitted to this clinical indignity in total silence. He kept one hand on her bottom as the other worked the hose clamp and he began to release the warm water into her bowels.

The water felt very hot to Susan and very shocking filling her tummy rapidly. She heard him adjust the clamp and knew that the flow had stopped momentarily.

He placed one hand under her tummy and felt its fullness. Her skin was silken to the touch. He cupped her bosom in his hand and squeezed it gently. Then he moved his hand down to her lower abdomen and pubic mound, which he placed his palm against and held firmly while releasing the clamp again.

"Remember what I said about coming," he warned her, paradoxically kneading her soft, blonde curls. Susan whimpered, on the very edge of a climax. Her tummy began to feel very full. He held his hand against it firmly as the hot water filled her.

"After you've taken the entire two quarts I'm going to remove the nozzle, reinsert the retention plug, take you across my lap and paddle the plug. Understand?"

"Yes," she squirmed involuntarily at the thought.

Anthony halted the infusion several more times to prevent sudden cramping but finally every drop had traveled down the white hose and into her bottom and he very carefully, holding her open firmly, withdrew the deflated bulb and nozzle from her rectum and lay them aside. Then he re-lubricated the rubber plug and holding her apart again, slowly inserted it deep inside her bottom. Next he lifted her off the table and carried her back to the recamier where he sat down with her across his lap and placed the hardwood spanking paddle close by.

Anthony took time to adjust her comfortably across his lap, making sure that the retention plug was firmly and deeply lodged between her pink cheeks.

"Your passivity is charming," he told her fondly, bending to kiss her ear and gently caress her smooth throat. "But I'm still irritated with you for that foolishness about Dennis," he added, taking up the small but solid paddle to begin the spanking.

Anthony brought the paddle down on either cheek several dozen times very sharply. Susan sobbed and wriggled on his lap but accepted the pain without protest. The fullness of her tummy and the sensation of the rubber plug embedded in her bottom all but cancelled out the pain. Particularly as he ceased to punish her satiny cheeks and began to apply the paddle instead to the base of the plug which divided her buttocks.

Susan enjoyed a shuddering climax six or eight swats into this segment of the paddling. Anthony held her fast as she spasmed, then quietly stroked and caressed her until she calmed down.

"All right, Susan, I'm going to let you up and leave you alone for awhile. But I'll expect you in my bedroom in one hour, freshly bathed and wrapped in that bridal gown set I sent you from Italy."

Less than one hour later Susan entered Anthony's bedroom, clad in a gown and wrapper of white fairy gauze, ribbons and lace. Anthony, who had been playing Gershwin tunes on his piano, which alerted Susan that he was in a happy mood, affected a stern demeanor when she stood before him for instructions.

"Well, young lady, what have you got to say for yourself?"

"I don't know," said Susan.

"Are you ready to give up this unseemly notion of seducing the chauffeur?"

"Not seducing. It was never that," she protested.

"It was that to the highest power," he informed her.

"I can't help it if Dennis adores me," Susan said, with a good deal more presence of mind than a girl who had just endured an examining room ordeal had a right to possess. "But I won't encourage him to do so."

"How magnanimous you are!" Anthony glared at her impertinence.

"But, just for the record, I never dreamed you'd take exception to my playing with Dennis. I expected it to be a trifle, beneath your notice."

"Just for the record, maybe it is, you irritating brat, but I'd prefer to stick with this particular fantasy for a while, wouldn't you?"

Susan couldn't resist climbing onto his lap then and covering his face and throat with kisses. He held her on his lap and suffered this attention with feigned ill humor.

"Stop it!" he ordered, firmly setting her on her feet once more. "I'm not done with you yet."

Susan blushed and waited.

"There's still your initial error of forgetting to come home all month to be punished," he reminded her.

"Oh," she meekly accepted this edict.

"I'm afraid I'm going to have to cane you," he told her coolly. Susan paled at this pronouncement and gazed at him wide-eyed, for he seemed serious.

Anthony got up, selected a charmingly brocaded little hassock and pushed it in front of the fire. A crack of thunder outside announced the resumption of the rain.

"Dispose yourself across this, Susan," her told her gravely. When she hesitated he took her by the arm and bent her over the ottoman himself, pulling the skirt of both her robe and dainty gown up to her waist. Susan's bottom had resumed its usual, creamy hue.

Susan lay exposed and trembling as he hunted through several closets for the English school cane he'd been saving for an occasion. But it wasn't where he had left it. In fact, the cane was gone. Anthony gazed at Susan's charming form, draped so provocatively across the hassock, with her long hair rippling down her back and wondered how he could have ever thought of caning her.

"Susan, what did you do with my cane?" he asked. Susan hung her head but made no answer. "I see," Anthony said, pacing around her. "You either hid or destroyed my English school cane, didn't you?"

Susan raised her head to follow him with her eyes.

"Well?" as he asked this question he unbuckled his belt, drew it from his trouser loops, wrapped the buckle end around his hand and administered the other to her bare bottom rather smartly several times. "What happened to the cane?"

"I threw into the incinerator," she admitted, craning her neck around to keep her eyes on the strap in his hand, but holding her position.

"Why did you do that, Susan?"

"Because I was afraid you would use it on me," she explained.

"All right, for that you're getting six of the best with my strap," he announced firmly.

Anthony went down on one knee beside her, placed one hand in the small of her back and began to strap her bare bottom soundly and with precision. Susan began to sob at once for the licking was hard and, in the context of their little universe, deserved.

"I'm very surprised at you, Susan. I thought you had better manners than that," he scolded. Then he held her in position, to rub the sting away, making her feel exposed and vulnerable. The palm of his left hand cradled her sex as he caressed her bottom.

"I went to a lot of trouble to get that school cane, Susan. The factory that made them no longer exists."

"I'll get you another and take the caning if you'll just forgive me," Susan promised.

"And where do you intend to obtain such an item?"

"Hugo can get one for me," she replied, turning to look at him.

"Another of your boyfriends!" Anthony stopped caressing to spank her.

"Ow! I'm sorry! He isn't a boyfriend at all though!" Susan protested.

"On the subject of boyfriends, young lady," Anthony pulled Susan up and sat her on the hassock while he stood up, "I'm going to give you some rules. First rule: when I'm in New York, you reside with me. Do you understand?"

"Yes, Sir," replied Susan, blushing at being told that she was wanted.

"Secondly, you can disregard what I said about you and Dennis before. You may amuse yourself with Dennis in whatever way you like while I'm out of town."

"Truly?"

"Your instinct was correct. I don't mind Dennis bonding to you. You need a body guard in this city."

"I see," Susan smiled.

"All right, get to bed," he ordered, dimming the lights almost completely and undressing. He climbed in beside her, made her face away from him and embraced her from behind, locking his arms around her tiny waist.

"I suppose that woman I saw you with tonight would have taken a caning?" Susan asked.

"I'm sure she would have," Anthony murmured, "if I paid her enough."

"Oh!"

"But thank you for reminding me about your shocking behavior in following me tonight!" Anthony rolled her onto her tummy and pulled back the voluminous covers and bedding. "Relax, I'm not going to spank you anymore. There are other ways to punish an overly curious little girl."

Susan bit her lip as he flourished a tube of hot lube before her eyes and broke the seal. She'd experienced the lubricant known as "lube" before but never the quick heating variety and felt both curious and afraid.

"Remember what I told you I was going to do?" Anthony asked her.

"Sodomize me?"

He allowed her to examine the lardlike lubricant and inhale its cinnamon scent. Then Anthony applied a very small amount to the tip of his finger and inserted it into her anus. Susan hid her blush in the pillows. Very quickly the area so treated began to radiate a not unpleasant warmth.

"I'm told that if you inadvertently apply too much of this stuff it can become most uncomfortable," he advised, massaging the stimulating ointment lightly between her cheeks. Then he withdrew his hand from this intimate area and stroked her bottom while she squirmed.

"My little Susan's such a naughty girl that I have to invent new ways to punish her," he lamented; gently dividing her cheeks to survey the area he intended to plunder. Because of his careful handling, she did not seem any the worse for the humiliations that had already been visited upon her bottom that evening. Spreading her open more fully, he took care to scrutinize the tiny ring, which had proven the portal to so much pleasure for them both. Susan wriggled feverishly and ground against the bed.

"Hold still," he warned, deliberately holding her bottom spread apart with one hand while slipping the other under her to press against her sex.

"I can't, you're driving me insane!" she cried.

"All right, calm down. Face the wall like before and press back against me," he instructed, allowing his large, commanding erection to rest between her warm, smooth buttocks. "Now young lady, I want you to reach back with your little hand and put it in yourself, at the proper angle for you," he ordered, firmly wrapping her hand around his shaft. After such a vast amount of teasing Susan was enormously anxious for their union and obeyed his last command with alacrity, placing his penis between her cheeks and attempting to insert it into her bottom. Once Anthony understood the angle she was indicating he gently withdrew her hand and continued the operation himself, while holding her well apart to ease the entry.

"What were you thinking of, following me?" An inch slid in and she gave a small sob.

"I'm sorry," she replied, grabbing onto pillows with both hands.

"And then you confessed. You must have wanted to be punished for that," he declared, inserting another inch of throbbing cock into her bottom.

"Yes, I guess I did," she whimpered.

"You deserve a much worse punishment than this for such outlandish behavior," he advised, plunging in yet another inch. Now she was open to him fully and he felt this in the subtle insinuations of her dear little bottom against his groin. "You're lucky I don't give you a bare bottom spanking in front of Dennis tomorrow morning before he drives us to Random Point."

"No!" Susan cried with spirit.

"What? You don't want me to turn you over my knee in front of our driver?"

"Oh!" Susan cried, in sudden ticklish rapture as he thrust his penis even further and filled her clinging glove completely with his cock. Firmly encircling her waist with one arm and placing the other palm directly upon her flat tummy, he began to fuck her slowly and soundly.

"Now, Susan," he instructed, "Just relax and don't contract. I want you open to me and that's all. Understand?" he demanded.

"Yes, Sir!" she shivered with excitement as his palm pressed down lightly on her belly and his cock gently throbbed within her rectal sheath. Next she felt him withdraw slightly only to re-lubricate his shaft with a quantity of sheer, slippery gel, which eased his re-entry in the most voluptuous manner imaginable. Susan was on the verge of climaxing now. And after these several hours of punishing her, so was Anthony.

"Susan, what did I tell you about contracting?" he slapped her hard on the thigh.

"I'm sorry," she whimpered, forcing herself to loosen her grip on her lover's penis and cling lightly about it instead, which effort in and of itself was inexplicably stimulating.

"This is what you need," Anthony observed, pulling her bottom cheeks firmly apart as his cock plunged in between them to the hilt. "You need to be controlled just like this," he pressed his palm against her tummy more firmly now as he slowly thrust his penis into her bottom. Susan made a valiant effort not to contract her bottom around the brave intruder, but inevitably determined to bring this rapturous torment to its logical conclusion by squeezing on his ramrod until she came.

The moment he felt Susan's internal spasms Anthony allowed himself the luxury of release within the warm, clinging recesses of her bottom. He himself had teetered so precariously on the edge of orgasm for the last hour or so, that he'd instituted the no-contraction rule simply to postpone his own climax until she had achieved her own. In doing so he had unwittingly stumbled on the single most arousing piece of foreplay for Susan, which was simply to force her to keep her bottom spread during an insertion. Not only had this minimized the abrasive side effects of anal sex, without lessening its intensity for him, but it had also distracted her to the point where she was able to accept the entire length of his organ without discomfort. Technically, this was close enough to count as a simultaneous orgasm for Susan and Anthony and the two of them basked in its romantic glow for some moments before disengaging, with his face buried in her hair and her luscious bottom nestled against his groin.

Susan looked back at him over her shoulder and said, "You do love me, don't you?"

"That would be putting it mildly," he told her, gently kissing the nape of her neck.

Chapter Two

Damaris Pays a Debt

After her separation from Michael, Damaris Flagg became absorbed in her work at Random Construction, where she now had her old position back as William Random's office manager.

To distract herself from thinking about Michael Flagg, she worked long hours and spent most of her free time at the gym. She was miserable, but was becoming more desirable every day.

Damaris had now become indispensable to William Random. She no longer wore tight suits and 4" heels to work, as in the old days, but rather dressed in jeans and tweeds and sweaters, with sensible little shoes, and wore her hair in a long, glossy black ponytail. She'd become sturdy and dependable. William admired her greatly now.

Yet William respectfully refrained from attempting to resume their love affair, which had ended several years before, around the time that Michael had first taken an interest in her. At the onset of autumn, he was content simply to appreciate her increased dedication and enjoy her platonic companionship over an occasional meal.

In recognition of her superior job performance William showered benefits on Damaris. He hired a maid for her and provided a generous expense account. Whatever services she needed, he paid for. And he also replaced her antique bug with a sleek new company car.

Between William and Hugo, Damaris was able to furnish Cobweb Cottage, as it was charmingly called. And William found his way over every weekend to do small repairs and installations until everything was perfect for her.

While the two of them were busily and virtuously working together, they began to shyly study each other.

William had become so thoroughly tamed since the departure of his wife, that he hardly dared pat his secretary's bottom. And then too, Damaris had become such a hardworking puritan that there was little one could feel superior to her about. She was hardly a frivolous child to be put across one's knee and spanked any more, William told himself soberly.

Meanwhile, Damaris began to feel a stirring inside her whenever William strode into a room. One day he was over doing work around her house. Damaris went out onto the small verandah overlooking Pigeon Cove and observed him, in his shirtsleeves, up on a ladder, installing a new porch light. He was a slender and gracefully muscular man with short black hair and a chiseled, intelligent face. He looked down at her and smiled. Her tummy suddenly filled with butterflies and she knew she was in love again.

Damaris felt this revelation with a mixture of pleasure and anxiety as she sank into a low wooden porch chair to gaze at the small patch of coast.

When she had first become attracted to William he had been newly married to Laura. He and Damaris had been drawn to each other, and had enjoyed an office love affair. Then came the dreadful mistake that had led to her dismissal and her subsequent involvement with Lt. Flagg.

Though they hadn't been in each other's arms in several years, Damaris had often wondered whether William still cared for her. The way he had prepared the house for her and Michael indicated that he did. And so did the way he was looking after her now. Obviously William needed a woman. Laura had left him on pleasant terms and they saw each other often, but clearly she did not intend to return to him.

Damaris tried to exorcise the seductive thoughts. She mustn't even think about such absolutes as being William's woman. What she really should be doing was dating. In the scene. Placing and answering ads.

"Are you placing and answering ads?" she suddenly asked William, when he came down off the ladder to test the new light.

"No, are you?"

"No, not yet," she said.

William sat down to enjoy the pleasing vista of cove, sea, sand and sky on a temperate autumn afternoon. While Damaris was bringing out coffee, he mused on why he hadn't placed an ad. He didn't like to admit this to Damaris, but due to the exuberant accessibility of Laura's sister, Susan and Laura's own occasional availability since their separation, William had not felt like a wholly abandoned man. More recently, of course, he had begun to take a renewed interest in Damaris and thoughts of making love to her now filled his head whenever she was near him. She was and always had been the most daintily feminine young lady he had ever met.

When she handed him his coffee he scrutinized her closely. Why had she made that remark about ads, if not to let him know that she was once more available?

"Why don't we take each other's photos and submit ads to Hugo's magazine?" William suggested, as an activity.

"Should we?"

"Definitely. You'll get a new boyfriend immediately."

"And you?"

"I managed to get Laura last time I had an ad," William's tone indicated an abiding admiration for his wife in spite of the fact that she had outgrown him.

They agreed to meet back at William's house that evening to take photos. William set up a seamless and lights for portrait shots. Damaris was wearing a sleeveless, cream silk sheath, sheer stockings and high heels.

She looked very alluring and it reminded him of the old days. There had been perhaps 5 encounters in total, each of them special and sweet. Damaris saw him staring at her and blushed.

William made a few minor adjustments and began to take pictures.

"Perhaps I shouldn't encourage you to place an ad," said William, surprising her into a gratifying expression.

"No?"

"Someone might take you away from me."

"Would you hate that?" she smiled.

"I'd hate it."

"Are you saying something?" she asked.

"I'm saying that maybe neither of us should place an ad."

After they shot a roll of film between them, William took her into the downstairs sitting room, where he made a fire and insisting on serving her tea himself. Damaris then shyly addressed him.

"William, do you ever think about the fact that there is unfinished business between us?"

"What do you mean?"

"A long time ago I did something very bad to you."

"Oh, that," William frowned momentarily.

"I've felt guilty about it for years. It's grieved me."

"It's all right," he told her, "I forgave you for that long ago."

"But I've never forgiven myself," she explained. "And I never will until my transgression has been punished, and by the one I wronged."

"You want me to punish you?" he asked, surprised and immediately aroused.

"Yes."

"Punish, as in spanking?"

"Yes, and for real."

"For real, huh?" William stuck his hands in his pockets and paced.

"You don't agree?" she asked timidly.

"I'm not sure," he folded his arms and looked at her steadily. "I was very angry with you at the time. As I recall, I was seriously contemplating pressing charges."

Damaris flushed deeply, realizing how tasteless her request might seem to a person of sensibility.

"Forgive me, my suggestion was entirely inappropriate," she raised her beautiful eyes to him.

"It isn't that, Damaris. You just took me by surprise."

"You see, I made a terrible mistake. I'm really not that way," she explained with painful sincerity, her heart suddenly throbbing with love for William Random.

"I know you aren't. And besides, you've been such a model young lady ever since."

"Whatever I do to make amends never seems adequate. I still feel so horribly guilty."

"Well, you needn't."

"I wouldn't feel right about going out with you unless we took care of this business between us first," she softly insisted.

William paced and considered whether it would be strictly ethical to comply with her wishes. Throughout his brief but pleasant marriage he'd managed to invent a number of sterling reasons for spanking his wife and had never run into trouble. However, the first time he gave her a serious spanking for a reason he considered truly valid, (her inexplicable aloofness upon his return from Bolivia), she left him, hurling accusations of "boor" and "bully" at his head. Happily, he'd restored a portion of her esteem by rescuing Laura from Hugo Sands on the night of her infamous caning, but she'd made him suffer greatly for his blunder and they had never fully reconciled since.

This case was much different, however. Here was Damaris practically begging to be exonerated from the guilt that had tormented her for years, and legitimately so. What she'd done was deeply reprehensible and she hadn't been made to answer for her misdeed in any way. William studied her pure, open face and wondered if there would be any harm in complying with her request.

"It's true that your betrayal was a grave disappointment to me," he declared coolly, deciding at that moment to be the martinet she needed him to be. She lifted her head at the sternness in his tone. "I also agree that you deserve to be punished by my hand. Therefore on Monday evening, after work, we'll settle this once and for all."

Damaris spent the entire weekend and all of Monday in a pleasurable state of anxiety. She had dressed for work that day in a little grey v-neck wool jumper over a pristine white blouse and black stockings with black pumps. Sensible of his role as disciplinarian, William wore a faultlessly tailored charcoal wool suit with a white shirt and silk foulard tie.

At six o'clock Damaris timidly entered William's office.

"Have you locked the door?" he asked, getting up from his desk and drawing the wooden blinds shut against the deepening November evening.

"Yes, sir."

William sat on the edge of his desk and appraised her, standing before him in the manner and virtual uniform of a schoolgirl.

"You know why you're here," he began.

Damaris nodded.

"When you came to me three years ago, Damaris, I gave you your first decent job. I was good to you. I trusted you. I even loved you. And how did you repay me?"

It was all so true that Damaris felt a lump rise in her throat.

"I betrayed you," she whispered.

"That's exactly right. You stole contract bids, from this very office where we're standing, and sold them to an unscrupulous competitor of mine for payoffs in cocaine. Didn't you, Damaris?"

"Yes, sir," Damaris hung her head.

"Why did you do that, Damaris?"

"I was a speed freak. I thought I needed it. Randy Price tempted me. There's no excuse for what I did."

"No, there surely isn't. Especially in view of the fact that you were also my lover at the time!" William snapped. Damaris paled at the sudden sternness in his tone and demeanor.

"I'd give anything to undo what I did," she declared passionately.

"Wasn't it lucky for you, Damaris, that Lt. Flagg was so completely spellbound by the curve of your behind that he neglected to arrest you for possession of cocaine?"

"Oh, yes!" she fervently agreed, as the thought of herself in jail filled her with untold horror.

"You know, it was Michael who beseeched me not to press charges," he informed her.

"He did?"

"Feel loved, Damaris. After he described the arrest procedure to me, I decided that even as bad as you were, I couldn't put you through that."

"Thank you!" she exclaimed, with glittering eyes.

"Now, three years ago, when all of this occurred, I was much too furious with you to deal with you on any level. However, when you were compelled to remind me of the incident the other day, I realized that I now am capable of punishing you, in a controlled manner, for your grave misdeed."

William went around his desk, opened the top drawer, and withdrew from it a thin, tooled, chestnut brown leather strap, 2" wide, and 12" long, fitted to a polished wooden handle. He went back around the desk to stand in front of her again.

"Extend your right hand, Damaris," he told her. "Palm up and hold it still."

Trembling, she put out her hand. Grasping her by the wrist of that hand, he drew back the strap and laid it across the palm of her hand hard. Tears sprang to her eyes immediately as she jerked her hand away in pain and fear.

"No, young lady, put your hand back out. I'm going to make sure that you never steal from me or anyone else again. Do you understand?"

"Yes," she gasped.

"You're getting 6 on each hand."

Damaris extended her hurt hand once more and turned her head away. Again the strap came down and the sensation was more painful that anything she could have imagined, though the scene from The Seventh Veil did not fail to flit through her mind.

"Look at me, Damaris. You're being punished," he forced her to meet his eyes before he brought the strap down a third time on her tiny hand. The next three strokes came rapidly and seemed so shockingly painful to Damaris that she felt her knees buckling under her and for a long moment she seemed to be falling very slowly and softly backwards. The next thing she knew, she was sitting on the floor and William was pulling her back up to her feet. She hadn't actually passed out, but a momentary wave of dizziness had caused her to reel away from the punishment.

"Stop that," he scolded her. "You can take this. Now give me the other hand."

Sobbing almost uncontrollably now, she offered her left hand for discipline. Again she turned her face away and hid it against her sleeve. Grasping her firmly by the wrist, William began the whole procedure again, administering the strapping as though he were a disinterested 19th century schoolmaster and she a recalcitrant ward of the state.

"You know you have this coming, Damaris," he told her, and continued to mete out the full count.

The strapping on her hands was the most painful corporal punishment Damaris had ever experienced, but although she wept, she also felt almost giddy with relief that her sin was finally being expiated. After this he would fully forgive her and she would finally forgive herself. That was the value of punishment. Through her entire marriage to Michael Flagg, she had never felt entirely happy or at peace. Though she worked very hard at her jobs and as a homemaker, she always felt as though she was on probation, because he had met her in the commission of a crime for which they both knew she had never been punished. She felt he could never respect her, having taken her up under such circumstances.

After completing the strapping on her hands, William allowed her to immediately escape to the bathroom to run them under cold water. Alone in there she stared at her flushed, tear streaked face in the mirror and at her pink hands. She looked disheveled but still pretty and very young for her 29 years. She knew she'd gotten through the worst of it. He had been very severe with her. A spasm of pleasure rippled through her tummy at this thought. She remained in this position for five minutes, and when she pulled her hands out and patted them dry, the pain was gone.

She dried her face and brushed her hair before returning to him, shy to the point of mortification. He made her show him her hands and seemed pleased that the discipline had caused no apparent damage.

"I'm afraid I'm going to have to spank you as well," he told her gravely, taking her over his knee as he sat on a broad, heavy, armless wooden chair, which he had brought forward.

William took the time to adjust her slender torso perfectly across his lap, smooth her skirt down over her small but shapely buttocks and gently rearrange her long, glossy black waves. It had been three years since he had had the divine pleasure of correcting this beautiful, small woman and he could not help but relish in her endearing submission. She lay across his lap in the posture of a passive little girl, which caused his penis to throb violently.

"Now, Damaris," he said, patting her bottom softly through her skirt, "I want you to understand that I didn't enjoy being so harsh with you just now. But I think you needed it."

"Yes, sir," she looked back at him with an adorable face.

"Damaris, if I didn't know you better I'd think you wore this school girl outfit to soften me up," he said, continuing to fondle her bottom, now by putting his hand up under her skirt to caress the cool, bare flesh of her thighs above her stocking tops.

"No," she disagreed, "I wore it to make you harder."

"Don't be impertinent," he warned, giving her a hard smack.

"Ow!"

"Ow is right. It's been a long time, hasn't it?" he refamiliarized himself with her perfectly rounded, though now quite muscular bottom by spanking her over her skirt a couple of dozen swats, until Damaris felt the warmth spread across the entire surface of her buttocks beneath her skirt and panties. Grasping the rungs of the chair with both hands she surrendered to the delirious pleasure of receiving a sound spanking from this handsome, kind and caring man. Spasms of excitement rippled through her tummy and pubic mound, which were pressed so flat against his rock hard thighs as he brought his hand down again and again on her upturned buttocks.

A spanking on the skirt contains a spontaneous glamour. It had always worked on Damaris like an aphrodisiac. How kind and loving he was to treat her like this. His hand coming down felt effective and stern, though the pain was not severe. She loved the way he held her, so firmly across his lap, with his hand locked upon her small waist.

"I remember your bottom being slightly more voluptuous than this," he remarked, finally pausing to lift her skirt. She helped him by raising herself up on his lap, allowed herself one look back at him. "You've lost quite a bit of weight, I think."

"Is it all right?" she asked timidly.

He ran his hand across the mounds of her bottom, now beautifully encased in a pair of sheer black briefs and framed by a matching black garter belt, which held up her sheer black hose. Working out and running had changed her hourglass figure into a more modern, athletic one. Her waist was tinier than ever, but now her bottom was almost slim, though it still jutted nicely and filled out the snug briefs to perfection.

"It's much prettier than I remember it," William approved, fitness being his only religion. "And I remember it being the prettiest bottom I'd ever seen." This unexpected bit of eloquence touched Damaris deeply and she cast him a grateful glance over one delicate shoulder. He paused in caressing her bottom to lean down and kiss her mouth. Then he pulled away and smoothed her hair back so as to fully reveal her profile.

Of mixed Puerto Rican descent, Damaris possessed the black hair and ivory complexion of a princess. The black nylon panties, so classically sheer, revealed the rosy tinge, which his hand had already imparted to her tender alabaster skin. He was frankly surprised by the lush hue of pink that the spanking had already produced.

"I wish I didn't have to do this, Damaris," he signed, "but you committed a crime and then got off Scott free. We both know that was wrong. We went on for a couple of years trying to ignore it, but now justice must be served." He slowly pulled her panties down to her upper thighs, laying bare her radiant bottom for the first time. She caught her breath as he did so. "Now, Damaris, you knew that I would have to pull your panties down to spank you properly, didn't you?"

"Yes," she murmured, fastening her eyes to the grey carpet and steeling herself for the first blow.

"This is going to hurt," he warned her, which caused her to emit an involuntary little sob. "You're getting fifty of the best," he informed her and immediately began to spank her, both harder and faster than before, in such a way that had her kicking and squirming on his lap almost at once. Each smack caused a cry of pain to issue from her lips. His hard, calloused, palm hurt much more on her bare bottom, which had already been made tender from the spanking on her skirt. William stopped after ten smacks.

"Damaris hold still and stop making a fuss. This is nothing compared to what you should get for what you did so take it and be grateful that you're getting off so lightly," he advised her sternly and commenced spanking her again. This time she concentrated all of her resolve on remaining in position and not crying out, though she couldn't prevent a whimper from escaping her lips every second or third smack. "You've been a very disappointing little girl," William scolded, while spanking her harder still. "You should be ashamed of yourself," he continued, laying on the final ten whacks, more slowly, but with even greater severity. By the time the last stroke fell, she had already dissolved into tears.

William pulled her panties back up and set her on her feet.

"Because of the gravity of your offense, additional penance is required," he informed the tearful submissive, who could not help but rub her well-marked bottom with both hands. "Get down on your knees, young lady," he told her, unzipping his trousers. "There's more to discipline than spanking," he said, pulling out his long, thick, circumcised penis. "Now behave like a proper penitent," he instructed. Damaris had never been asked to give him head before and it had also been years since she had seen his large cock, therefore she approached it as gingerly as she would a wild woodland creature.

"Just a minute," he stopped her as she began to reach for him. "Go and get the strap I used on your hands and bring it here to me." Damaris obeyed him quickly, bringing him the school strap and then getting back into position. Grasping the strap by the handle he leaned forward in the chair and allowed her to capture his penis between her small, soft and so recently punished hands and bring it to her full, red mouth. William pulled her skirt up in back and laid the strap against her sheer black panties.

For a few moments he let her play with the knob of his cock, licking it and encircling it with her tongue. Then he pulled it out of her mouth and raised her chin to make her look at him.

"Haven't you ever given head before?" he asked her.

"Yes," she replied, wide eyed. "But not frequently."

"Apparently not," he snorted, leaned forward and applied the strap to her bottom hard three times as she hid her face against his shirtfront. Then he pulled away and placed his cock between her hands once more.

"Suck it this time," he told her coolly. Humiliated and aroused, Damaris opened her mouth to accept his large cock and did her best to honor it. "That's a good girl," he told her. "If you keep it wet and work it up and down with your hands, you'll find it much easier," he recommended, allowing the strap to fall to the ground. For a full five minutes he allowed her to struggle with his swollen organ, of which she was able to enfold perhaps a third within her small mouth. At last he said, "Are you going to be a good girl for me now?" She nodded, looking up at him with enormous eyes. It was enough. He had every intention of ejaculating into her mouth, but the white blouse and grey jumper stopped him. "Take it in your hands now," he told her, suddenly pulling free. With her darling little hands wrapped around him, pumping his slick engine fast, a copious flow of white lava erupted forthwith from his cock. It was such a large amount, indeed, that he was very glad he hadn't gagged his little friend with it.

In a moment, when he had recovered, he stuffed his still hard dick back into his trousers and made himself decent again. He then helped Damaris to her feet and told her to go and wash her hands. When she returned to him he motioned her to his desk.

"Now then, young lady, since you look like such a proper little school girl today, I want you to sit down and write me an essay, of 100 words or less entitled, 'What Really Excites Me' by Damaris Perez Flagg."

Damaris was extremely surprised by this command but hastened to take a seat behind the desk. She took a pen and paper and began to think while he paced with his hands in his pockets. Both of them were calm and very happy at that moment. Almost immediately Damaris handed the paper to him. At first it made him smile, then, recollecting his role, he cleared his throat and sternly frowned at her.

"Is this the kind of essay an honor student turns in?" He lay the paper down on the desk. Only two words appeared in her precise script, 'Anything anal.'

"Try again," he advised; "and this time, be more explicit."

"Must I? It's...rather embarrassing," she squirmed.

"Make the attempt anyway. It's for your own good, I assure you," he promised.

"Very well," she complied, chewing on the end of her pen before writing again. He lounged on a leather sofa while she worked, thinking how youthful she looked, with her trusting heart-shaped face and girlish body.

Finally she was satisfied and shyly placed the essay in his hand. Without looking at it he folded up her secrets and put them in his pocket.

"You can go home now, Damaris. I'll call on you later this evening. All right?"

"Yes, William. Thank you."

"And Damaris, I think we'll keep the photos we took today for our album instead of submitting them to Hugo. You don't need to place an ad. I'm sure I can take care of all of your needs."

Vanilla incense perfumed the air of Cobweb Cottage, when William arrived there that night. Since seeing her he'd gone home, fed his cats, showered, changed into more casual clothes and read her little essay, which worked like an aphrodisiac on him in seconds. It was apparent to William, who now paid attention to such things as women's moods, that a great change had come over Damaris in the past few days. The subtle sadness that had lingered about her since leaving her husband had been replaced by a shy and hopeful anticipation. He noticed she was smiling and giggling again. And today she had even made an impertinent remark. He realized that he hadn't seen her this merry in years, and wondered whether it was indeed the weight of the crime on her conscience or the oppressive influence of an overly strict husband which had subdued her natural ebullience this long while.

Her essay had been quite exciting to read.

"Ever since early childhood," it began, "I have been enthralled by the idea of anal discipline. Forced examinations, temperature taking and rectal penetration have figured largely in my fantasies.

Enema equipment fascinates me. The setting may be clinical, but the enema must be administered for punishment rather than health or hygiene, and always in conjunction with spanking.

I have longed to meet a man who would humiliate me gently, to teach me self-control. Strict discipline plays a role in all of my fantasies.

I must mention that my favorite position is across William Random's knee."

It was difficult not to smile all through dinner. It appeared that he was beloved again, and by an exceptional girl. Whatever nagging doubts he might have had about her trustworthiness had long ago disappeared. Though he now agreed with Damaris that the punishment she had requested was necessary, both to ease her troubled conscience and gracefully reestablish him as her dominant. Her charming essay, which he congratulated himself on requesting, provided unexpected thrills, which he pondered the entire time they were apart.

Damaris also could not get the essay out of her mind. She'd memorized it as she wrote it and now wondered which of her statements he would choose to explore. William had changed for the better since being abandoned by his wife. He seemed more sensitive now. Wasn't the whole idea of the essay calculated to find out how to make her happy? Damaris thrilled to think she finally had a man who really cared. And the fact that he was her first love in the scene, the first man who had ever really spanked her, filled her with romantic contentment.

Damaris had changed into a winter white woolen dress with a nipped waist and full, round skirt. Her belt and accessories were light brown. The light beige stockings she had on led to a profusion of white ruffled lingerie, which William hoped to admire shortly. If his eye did not deceive him, she had a full corset on under her dress to further define her already small waist. She'd put her hair into a long, smooth ponytail, bound by a flower. Pearl teardrops hung from her ears and encircled her throat. She looked a perfect lady in her dainty 3" pumps.

She had a small, beautifully prepared vegetarian meal ready for him, which he consumed quickly and appreciatively. She couldn't stop blushing.

After she had cleared away the dishes, she paused in the doorway to watch him putting more logs on the fire. When he got to his feet he motioned her over to him and then made her sit beside him on the carved, cream upholstered antique recamier with which Hugo Sands had endowed the cottage.

"I want you to know, Damaris," he took her hands in his, "that I've given a great deal of thought to your essay and I've come to one immutable conclusion."

Damaris made no reply but dropped her gaze, feeling her face grow hotter.

"Would you like to hear what it is?"

"I think so," she timidly ventured.

"I've decided that the only way to control your deviant tendencies is to force you to experience all of them."

"You have?" she looked at him with wide eyes and a pounding heart.

"Yes, because it will do you good."

Damaris tried to get up and run away but he caught her wrist and yanked her back down.

"Are you afraid?"

"Yes."

"Don't worry," he patted her hand reassuringly, "we'll start small. Anyway, I'm going to need some time to create the proper environment for your needs."

"Oh. Good!"

"I wish you hadn't let Michael take the house after I'd put in all of those modifications just for you," William suddenly observed with irritation.

"I'm sorry," she murmured.

"I'm going to punish you for that," he warned her.

"You are?"

"Do you see these?" he showed her a bunch of keys on a stainless steel ring. "They're keys to my friend Dr. Grindle's office. I've done him a couple of favors over the years and now he's doing me one. His office will be empty tonight. We're going there now."

William helped her into camel reefer coat and beret and led her out to his car. The doctor's office was in the neighboring town of Woodbridge, 4 miles up the coast. It was located on the second floor of a wooden Victorian triple-decker with bay windows overlooking Elm Street. There was a broker on the first floor and a custom tailor on the third. Both went home at six, and the doctor departed even earlier. They were in the three-square block heart of the business district of downtown Woodbridge and at 9 pm there wasn't a soul on the pavement or in a storefront.

"I've brought my own equipment, some of it purchased on Dr. Grindle's advice." William explained, showing her a leather satchel.

"But, what did you tell him?" she asked, her cheeks burning with mortification as they went up the old-fashioned wooden banister staircase.

"Simply that I knew a young lady who had a fantasy of making love on an examining table. Actually, Dr. Grindle fancies himself kinky because once had me install a mirror above his bed, so he gave me a knowing wink with the key."

They entered the office of the doctor and then William locked them in. He took her through the waiting room and consultation room and then into the first examining room, which had many of the original fixtures from the 1930's, when the apartment was remodeling to accommodate a medical practice. Bottle green leather upholstery against heavy mahogany furnishings along with potted palms and thick Venetian blinds created a secure and ambient environment for the timid patient.

William adjusted the central heating to warm the examining room. On a marble topped counter Damaris noticed a box of rubber gloves, a bundle of cellophane wrapped thermometers, and a jar of petroleum jelly.

"Damaris, remove all of your outer garments, including your dress."

Damaris hastened towards the screen of white muslin stretched on a mahogany frame.

"No, dear, change where I can see you," he corrected her mildly. Blushing, she stripped off her white woolen dress and stepped out of it, revealing her charms to him in the daintiest white brocade corset he'd ever seen. The corset had a built in décolleté bra which presented her heavenly cleavage to perfection. A pair of white satin bikinis covered a small portion of her bottom.

"Lie face down on the examining table, Damaris," he told her, removing his jacket and rolling up his sleeves. Damaris obeyed, watching him wash his hands at the marble sink and break the open the cellophane of one of the thermometers. She hid her face in her hands and waited, feeling herself becoming wet between her legs. She had never felt so humiliated in her life. His cool efficiency made it almost unbearable. Her clit ached madly. She pressed against the table to sooth it, but then an even worse outrage occurred. He pulled her panties down to just below her bottom and left her there. Then he went to get some lubricant.

"Fantasies are very pleasant, Damaris," he told her, "but some prove uncomfortable when they come true." He came back and divided her buttocks gently with his fingers. "Just relax and let me examine you now," he warned sternly. "I want you open. Do you understand?"

"Yes," she whispered, trying to go limp.

"You're going to have your temperature taken now," he told her, lubricating her bottom liberally, "and you're going to hold still while I do it."

The thermometer felt very cold going in. She couldn't help but squirming in an ecstasy of shame.

"Didn't I tell you to hold still?" he slapped her bare bottom sharply.

"I'm sorry!"

He adjusted her thighs so that they were together and allowed her to contract her bottom around the thermometer, which he'd inserted to the hilt.

"Lie there and don't move a muscle or you'll get a good paddling."

Damaris groaned. He walked around in front of her and leaned against a counter top, checked his wristwatch and folded his arms.

"Remember what I said about moving," he warned. "You're here to learn about self control."

Damaris tried to hold still. The old-fashioned mantelpiece clock ticked off the seconds loudly. Finally he went around behind her again to remove the thermometer.

"98.6" he said. "Therefore there's no reason we can't continue with the procedure." He gave her a reassuring pat on the bottom and began to undo the long row of hooks and eyes that fastened her glove tight corset up the back. "This perfect little corset is much too constricting for what I have in mind for you, young lady," he told her, unhooking her stockings from the garters, removing her pumps and hose and the lowered bikinis, then laying open the corset to reveal her slim waisted nude torso as she continued to lie face down on the table. He made her lift up to pull the corset free then neatly folded it and lay it aside. Next he rolled her over so that she lay on her back, whereupon he leaned down momentarily and kissed her on the mouth. "Are you going to behave?" he asked her.

"Yes," she replied, trembling with a sudden shiver.

"I'll make it a little warmer in here," he told her. On his way back he grabbed the black satchel, opened it on a rollaway table adjacent to the leather examining table and brought out several items, which Damaris viewed with a mixture of excitement and shame.

"I went to a medical supply store this afternoon and had a nice long talk with the proprietor," William explained, bringing out a cylindrical, bottle green hot water bag and a length of thick white hosing along with a tapering 4" nozzle. "I told him that my wife had been advised by her holistic doctor to take a therapeutic enema once a week and she had asked me to administer it. He noticed my fascination at the thickness of this particular hose and explained that it was called a colon tube and while it was usually reserved for high colonics - I'll explain what those are later - it could also be adapted into a regular enema with excellent results."

The next item William removed from the satchel was a standard, hard plastic 6" vibrator.

"Spread your legs, Damaris," he said, delicately dividing the lips of her vagina with his fingers. "This is part of your discipline," he told her, gently inserting the vibrator into her pussy, which was creamy wet from her excitement and pushing it almost all the way in. She caught her breath as he took her with the cold object. Taking care to leave the hilt of the vibrator exposed about an inch, he pressed his palm down lightly on her flat tummy, which made the vibrator inside her feel even more naughty.

"You're going to be completely filled," he told her. "Do you understand?"

"Yes."

"Good girl. Now roll over on your tummy again."

When Damaris obeyed her spread her bottom cheeks and lubricated her anus again.

"Now lie still until I tell you to do otherwise," he recommended, checking to see that the dildo was still firmly lodged in her vagina before filling the hot water bottle.

"This water will be very warm, Damaris," he told her; coming back and suspending the bottle from an IV stand by the examining table. "The colon tube is thicker than a normal enema hose. It's meant to go all the way into the colon, up to 24", according to the pharmacist. Now, since I'm not a doctor, I'm not going to attempt such an ambitious insertion. We'll save that for another time, after I've studied up."

"Why does it have to go in so deep?" she asked.

"I'm glad you're paying attention," he said, smiling slightly at her curiosity "The idea behind a double colonic is to have two tubes going into the patient's bottom simultaneously. One goes deep and one shallow. One carries the water in, the other carries it out. I'm told the entire procedure can take up to two hours, the objective being a deep and thorough cleansing."

Damaris could not imagine anything so perverse being sanctioned by the medical profession.

"This time, however, we're just going to do a single tube and insert it only as deeply as it feels comfortable for you," he told her. "Now get up on your hands and knees and spread your legs," he pushed down on the small of her back to make her bottom jut more pertly. He also tapped the hilt of the vibrator back. "This is to remain firmly lodged in your vagina throughout the procedure. Do you understand?"

"Yes, but it's so slippery!"

"If you let it pop out I'm going to be very harsh with you," he promised, causing her to sob. "It's time you realize you're being punished."

William now donned rubber gloves and inserted his longest finger in her spread bottom as far as it would go. Damaris whimpered. "You're ready," he declared, removing finger and gloves. "Now, Damaris, I don't know if you noticed before, but if you turn your head slightly to the left you can see a mirror over the marble sink which reflects a mirror positioned behind you. Therefore, if you care to observe what's happening to you, you may do so."

"Oh no!" she cried.

"Very well. Now thrust your bottom well up and separate your knees and widely as possible. I don't want to have to tell you that again," he tapped the vibrator back a fraction of an inch into her pussy and spreading her cheeks once more he inserted the lubricated nozzle of the colon tube into her anus very slowly until it all disappeared. Damaris whimpered and shut her eyes as she felt the gentle but determined invasion. She was overcome by shame almost to the point of dizziness. After the nozzle had completely disappeared he paused and adjusted the angle of the hose depending from her bottom, making sure it was placed as high as possible. "Now, Damaris, I'm going to insert a small amount of the hose into your bottom, because it will do you good to feel it. But you're going to have to tell me the moment it becomes uncomfortable. All right?"

"Yes," she promised.

Fully lubricating three or four inches of rubber tubing, he began to gently insert it. At first it did not hurt in the slightest, though it was the most humiliating experience she had ever endured to hold herself open for the hose. Then finally the nozzle seemed to butt up against an inner wall and she cried out in distress. Immediately he pulled a half inch of hose back out.

"Good girl," he complimented her. "Is that comfortable enough?"

"Yes, I think so," he replied, daring for the first time to look in the mirror. The sight of her slim, smooth bottom so lewdly divided and penetrated by the sterile medical apparatus was excruciatingly exciting. William walked around her, making minor adjustments and tapping the vibrator into her pussy.

"All right, Damaris, I'm going to administer the enema now," he told her, keeping one hand on the curve of her bottom while releasing the hose clamp with the other. "We'll start with half, let you rest, then finish."

Immediately very warm water gushed into her tummy, and again, the shock of penetration made her momentarily dizzy with a mixture of embarrassment and pleasure. As if reading her mind, William placed his hand under her belly as the warm water filled it and said, "I'm sorry that I have to embarrass you like this, but it's the only way you'll remember the lesson." He closed off the clamp and gently squeezed her tummy, then her pubic mound, which was drenched. "Why on earth are you so wet?" he asked in surprise, showing her his hand, which glistened with her moisture. Damaris hung her head. "You'll take the rest of the enema now," he told her firmly. It did not take long to administer the full two quarts. Damaris squirmed during the procedure, which nearly caused the vibrator to slip out.

"You're not doing a very good job holding onto this," he told her, pulling it out entirely and laying it to one side. When the last drop had been filtered into her bottom William made Damaris lie flat on the table, on her full tummy, to slowly withdraw the thick colon tube from her bottom. Damaris bit her knuckle throughout this protracted operation, teetering on the edge of climax. Finally the nozzle was removed from her bottom and William took away the entire apparatus and deposited it in the sink. Damaris lay on her tummy and waited for him without moving a muscle.

When he returned to her he took up and relubricated the vibrator.

"Damaris, didn't I tell you to keep the vibrator in place?"

"I tried to!"

"Never mind that. Get your legs apart." He spread her buttocks and inserted the rounded tip of the vibrator into her anus then slowly plunged it up into her rectum to the hilt. Now he pressed her thighs and cheeks together. Once he had her flat against the leather table and plugged, he removed a leather paddle from the satchel and showed it to her.

"Now then, young lady, I would like you to retain the enema for 20 minutes. If for some reason you can't manage to do this, you're to tell me. Understand?"

"Yes, sir."

"Are you cramping?"

"No, sir."

"Good. Now bury your face in your hands and think about why this is happening to you," he said, bringing the paddle down on her bottom, across the crack and vibrator hilt. "This is happening because you've been a very wicked girl," he told her, smacking her firmly again. She sobbed and ground against the table.

"Lie still," he told her. "I want you to take your punishment. I'll be very angry with you if you have an orgasm now." Naturally she almost came at these words and forced herself to make her mind a blank. "This position is obviously too comfortable for you," he observed, lifting her up by the hips. "Get your bottom up in the air and spread your knees apart as far as they will go. Head down," he told her briskly.

Now when he stood beside her he could run his hand under her tummy and squeeze her luscious triangle below it. Her small tummy felt very full and smooth under his hand. She was breathing quickly, as though she were greatly affected by all that was happening to her.

Now, to further torment her, he began to work the dildo out of her bottom hole, and alternately paddle it back in. Then he paused, put the paddle down and had a look at her face to make sure she was all right.

"This is for your own good, dear," he promised, brushing her hair off her face. "You know, Damaris, this is the way they used to deal with willful children in the old days. When a little girl was insolent, she might receive a sound spanking across her papa's lap and a hot enema, to purge her of her naughtiness."

"Now remain in that position while I set the equipment to rights," he instructed, leaving her with her bottom in the air, her flushed face pressed against the table.

William thoroughly washed and dried all of the apparatus he'd used and packed them away into the satchel again. Perhaps ten minutes had passed since administering the enema and as yet she felt no discomfort.

Pulling a straight-backed chair into the center of the room he took Damaris off the table and seating himself on the chair, he carefully laid her across his lap without disturbing the vibrator, which was still deeply buried in her rectum.

"Now I know that you have a very full tummy, and this probably isn't the most comfortable position for you, but you're going to have to be spanked tonight as part of your discipline."

"I understand," she said timidly.

William began to spank her mildly, just enough to raise the color in her cheeks. He spanked around the plug this time, until the entire surface of her bottom was pleasantly warm to her and she was writhing on his lap.

"Hold still, dear," he warned, sensing her mounting excitement. He still wanted to add one more refinement to her torments before allowing her to climax. "I don't want any squirming out of you," he told her, picking up the paddle and smacking her hard across the butt of the vibrator. Restraining her firmly across his lap with a hand clamped to her waist, he applied the paddle to the plug repeatedly and vigorously at least ten times before laying it aside. Damaris sobbed with emotion.

"Good girl," he told her, pulling the hilt slightly out of her bottom in order to twist the buzzing mechanism on. The moment he started the vibrator she began to squirm. He shut it off and smacked her sternly on either side of the plug. "No, Damaris. I told you to hold still. Didn't I?"

"I'm sorry, I didn't think you meant then too," she explained.

"Well I did."

"I'm sorry."

"All right. Now I'm going to turn the vibrator on again. And when I do I want you to simply contract your bottom around it and hold your position. Do you understand?"

"Yes."

William flipped the vibrator on and holding her fast across his lap began to firmly spank her bottom while she obediently clenched the pulsing invader between her cheeks. Before a minute had elapsed she was overcome by the spasms of a remarkably satisfying climax, the likes of which she hadn't known since Michael had once or twice subjected her to similar indignities.

Damaris was then allowed to depart with her clothes into the bathroom; wherein she remained for some time while William restored the room to its original state of tidiness.

When she emerged, looking flushed and abashed, back in the white dress and neat leather pumps, William was charmed by her appearance.

"Come on, young lady, I'll take you home and tuck you in," he said, taking her hand and leading her out of the office.

In the car she couldn't look at him, while he looked at her now and then with a friendly smile.

"Damaris why are you so quiet?" he finally said.

"Embarrassed," she murmured, staring out the window at the autumnal splendor of the village outskirts in the moonlight.

"Would it make you feel better if I told you that the scene we did tonight was the most exciting thing I've ever done with a woman?"

Damaris looked at him. "I don't believe you," she said.

"You don't want to believe me. You're probably afraid that I'll insist on subjecting you to such treatments regularly."

When they arrived at Cobweb Cottage William insisted that Damaris get into bed immediately while he made her a cup of tea.

When he brought it to her she sat up under the covers in a tailored Christian Dior nightshirt, with her long black hair loose. She took a few sips to please him then lay back on the pillow as a soft drowsiness overcame her.

"Will you stay with me tonight?" she asked, extending her small hand to him. She was asleep before he'd finished undressing.

Chapter Three

Susan's Senior Year

Susan Ross began her senior year at Barnard, but after she was mugged in broad daylight on the Morningside Heights campus during the first week of October, Anthony Newton convinced her to transfer to college upstate for the remainder of the year.

At that time in their relationship, the only thing Anthony enjoyed more than seeing Susan on weekends and holidays, was receiving her letters. Susan wrote her lover continuously, with her impressions of the school, the professors, the characters in the lesbian girl gang which she had been absorbed into, and especially her fantasies.

However, Anthony, who was himself a scholar, knew Susan was not spending enough time on her studies because of their correspondence. And he took her to task accordingly on a visit to her in November.

They were leaning on the railing of the wooden bridge that spanned Vassar Lake, staring at the burnished reflection of leaves in the wind-rippled water. It was about three in the afternoon, chilly and overcast.

"Susan, I love your letters, but you can't keep spending so much time writing me," he told her fondly, rubbing her small, leather gloved hand against his cheek.

"Why not?" she pulled him by the hand over the bridge and onto the path into the woods, where they began to walk. The floor was soft with pine needles and fallen logs were everywhere.

"I'm sure you're not studying enough, Susan," he scolded. "You're spending too much time on frivolous diversions, like girl gangs and letters home. I notice you're even sending a weekly letter to Dennis!"

he referred to his young English driver, who was devoted to Susan and had been heartbroken since she went away.

Susan blushed at this last remark.

"Am I not supposed to do that?" she asked.

"That's depends on what you're writing. But why you should have anything to write to my chauffeur is a mystery to me," he endeavored to sound stern.

Anthony waited until they had walked another ten minutes before stopping in the woods.

"Get over here, young lady," he took her by her arm to the perfect fallen trunk, sat down on it and turned her over his knee. "But, what did I do?" she asked as his hand came down on the seat of her tweed skirt.

"You argued about the letters," he said, giving her a brisk spanking.

"But, I can't not write you!"

"You can write shorter letters and study more," he smacked her soundly, holding her firmly across his lap by her little waist. "And you can stop flirting with my driver!" He pulled up her skirt and smacked her on the panties, which were white cotton. "What kind of letters are you writing Dennis, anyway? Mistress letters?"

"Was I not supposed to do that?" she gave him an adorable look over one shoulder.

"You're a very bad girl," he told her sternly and pulled down her panties. "I'm going to have to spank you on the bare bottom for that."

"No! It's too cold out here!" she cried, trying to pull her panties back up.

"You won't feel cold for long," he promised her and proceeded with the spanking.

The smacks sounded much louder when administered to her creamy, white, bare bottom, but they were completely alone in the woods except for the squirrels and birds and neither of them felt concerned about the noise. Anthony concluded the spanking with twelve of the best and then let her set herself to rights.

"Speaking of correspondence, Susan," he said, "that was an extremely wicked letter you wrote me the other day."

In the letter he referred to, Susan had revealed a guilty fantasy, which she had nurtured for years, but never dared try to fulfill. She looked at him, blushing and rubbing her bottom. He got up and they began to walk again.

"Do you really think it's wicked?" Susan asked him, almost dizzy with excitement from the brief spanking.

"No. It would only be wicked if I were your real life daddy. However, it's probably no accident that you only fall in love with men who are old enough to be your father."

"I guess that's true," she said. Anthony had just entered his 40's. Sherman Cooper, the executor of her estate and her uptown lover, was in his middle thirties. Hugo Sands, her mentor in the scene and occasional playmate, was in his middle forties. William Random, her brother in law and sometimes lover, was also in his middle 30's. Susan would turn 21 that year. "But I don't think of you as my father," she hastened to explain. "You're so boyish and charming. My father wasn't anything like you. They're not making older men the way they used to."

Susan had explained in her letter that she longed to experience a scene in which she was spanked like a helpless little girl.

"I'll tell you what, Susan. Tonight, at the inn, after dinner, you can bring me your report card. All right?"

Duchess County was filled with bed and breakfast inns and Anthony Newton had booked connecting rooms for Susan and himself in one of the prettiest and oldest of them for that weekend. In her room, after dinner, Susan changed into a navy pleated skirt and white blouse, white knee sox and burgundy oxfords.

She knocked on Anthony's door timidly but slipped inside quickly, a beautiful young lady, with wavy, long, dark blonde hair. Anthony had managed to obtain a room with a piano and he was playing some delicate etude of Chopin when she entered, which gave her a thrill.

Anthony rose from the bench and managed to look very serious upon her arrival.

"Well, it's about time you got home, young lady. Did you hope that if you stayed away long enough I might forget that you were bringing your report card home today?"

Susan was speechless with embarrassment. She had never actually entered into a play-acting situation with Anthony before and felt suddenly very intimidated about the whole idea. And yet, she had prepared a report card. Unable to think of what else to do, she handed it to him.

Anthony sat down in a large wing chair by the fireside. Ordering her to sit upon a hassock by his side, he consulted the paper. Susan had printed it out on the Mac in her dorm room. At the top it said: Gramercy Park Middle School. Then below that it said: Susan Ross, 7th grade. First Semester. Teacher: Mr. Elgarten. Then came her grades: Art 98%, English 92%, Social Studies 80%, General Science 74%, Music 68%, Algebra 65%, French 64%, Physical Education 66% And under the section for remarks, Mr. Elgarten had commented: Susan is a nice girl, but she often talks in class and distracts the other children. Susan should apply herself more and bring her up grades in French and Math.

Anthony looked up at Susan sternly. Suddenly she felt weak. These were her actual marks from her seventh grade class, first semester class, which she could never forget as it was the first time she had ever failed anything.

"Susan, this is very disappointing. Some of these grades are shocking, considering your intelligence. You've actually managed to fail French."

Susan hung her head.

"Susan, do you remember the last time you brought home a poor report card to me? We had a talk then and I told you what would happen if you continued to disgrace yourself with marks like this. Do you remember what I said?"

Susan merely shook her head.

"I said that if you didn't show an improvement by your next report card that I would give you a good spanking."

Susan looked at him with wide eyes. He got up, took her by the wrist and led her to a heavy, wooden straight-backed chair, which he had placed in the center of the Tudor style wood beamed room.

"Imagine a daughter of mine getting 68% in music!" said Anthony indignantly, while turning her over his knee. "You're a very bad little girl," he informed her, smacking the seat of her skirt very firmly several dozen times.

"Why are your grades so poor, Susan?" he paused in the spanking to ask her.

"I don't know," she murmured, only aware of the hot flashes of excitement which flooded her tummy.

"I'll tell you why. It's because you're an idle, spoiled brat who'd rather read Mad magazine than do her homework," he decided, flipping up her skirt and commencing the spanking all over again on the seat of her white nylon panties. These panties were so sheer that the pinkness of her well-spanked bottom glowed through the material to entice him.

"Don't fuss," he paused in the spanking to warn her. "You're going to be punished." He pulled her panties down to mid thigh and renewed his grip on her tiny waist before bringing his palm down vigorously on her bare bottom.

Anthony's hand descended firmly and rhythmically several dozen times, reddening both her cheeks thoroughly with inexorable determination. Susan kicked and squirmed across his lap but didn't cry out, mindful of their situation within the inn. He had to hold her little hand by the wrist to prevent it from covering her pink, vulnerable bottom towards the end of the spanking.

"Aren't you ashamed of yourself?" he demanded.

"Yes," she sobbed, on the verge of real tears from the emotion of the scene.

"Yes, what?"

"Yes, Daddy," she replied.

Anthony tucked his arm around under her waist for increased control over her lithe, little body.

"And as if the poor grades weren't bad enough, I also have to hear from Mr. Elgarten that you've been rude enough to talk in class. That makes me very angry, Susan. I thought I taught you better than that." Anthony continued to spank her slowly and firmly, alternating cheeks, until her entire bottom had been stained a deep magenta by his hand. "Lie still, young lady," he ordered when she gave a little kick at an especially hard whack. "You're not going anywhere until I'm satisfied you've been properly corrected."

Susan felt as much like a child as she ever needed to feel. She was aware of his hand on her waist and the clock ticking on the mantelpiece. The spanking was becoming harder and she had begun to feel uncomfortably sore, though the actual smacks were continuing to stimulate her.

Anthony soon found himself embracing the spirit of the fantasy. When he caught his own reflection in the mirror he was amused by the determined compression of his lips as he continued to sharply apply the palm of his hand to Susan's round, upturned bottom.

"I never want to see another report card like that again," he warned, finishing the licking with a hard, fast, dozen swats. Then he helped her up off his lap and pulled her panties back up. She turned away from him and hid her face. "Now go to your room," he told her sternly.

When she entered her own room she threw herself face down on the bed and attempted to still the pounding of her heart. With her bottom so warm and sore it was easy to imagine that she really was a little girl who got a spanking from her handsome, young daddy.

She lay there fantasizing until Anthony came in and slipped into the large feather bed beside her. She snuggled into his arms and laid her fair head against his chest.

"You make me so happy," she confessed. He picked up a plush brown Peter Rabbit in a blue coat she'd had in bed with her.

"Susan Ross, I've never known you to sleep with a stuffed animal," he teased her fondly, locking her in his arms from behind, so that her now cool bare bottom was pressed against his now very hard cock.

"But when I was eleven I did," she confessed, grinding back against him.

"Those were your real grades, weren't they, Susan?"

"Yes," she admitted with some embarrassment. "I failed French."

"Just be thankful I wasn't your father the day you brought home a 68 in music," Anthony sternly declared.

Susan sighed.

"When I was eleven," Anthony told her, "I greatly admired a little girl named Jill. We were part of the same after school clique and it got to the point where I walked her home from school every day and very often kissed her. She also let me put my hand into her blouse and squeeze her bottom under her skirt.

However, Jill was a fresh little girl and one day she took it into her head to make me jealous. She let my friend David walk her home from school that day and pitched bottle caps with him all afternoon in the street.

I was furious. I had my usual piano lesson at 4:30 and I remember that was the first day I stumbled all the way through the Rhapsody in Blue. At 5:30 I ran over to her block and was lucky enough to see Jill playing potsy with two or three girlfriends from our class. We all had to get home for dinner within the half hour but I was able to call Jill away from the other girls and induced her to take a walk around the block with me.

There was a vest pocket park on the way and I stopped at our favorite bench. The one where she used to let me kiss her. We had it out then and there. I told her that she had made me angry walking home with David and spending time with him all afternoon instead of me. Then, Susan, I actually told her that I was going to spank her. She looked at me and didn't run away. Then she let me pull her across my lap and swat the seat of her skirt at least six times. When I let her up she immediately kissed me, and then ran away. I think I masturbated for the first time that day. She stayed my girl friend all summer after that, though I never dared attempt another spanking."

Absence inflamed Susan's passion for Anthony. When a weekend came when they couldn't be together because of his commitments, she became cross and unreasonable. And when she was told that Anthony would be in London during Thanksgiving week, the first big school holiday of the year, she sulked and cried. Anthony was surprised, touched and annoyed. She had never taken on like this before about trips abroad, which occurred frequently in his life.

Before departing for England, Anthony made time to drive up to Poughkeepsie. He found her in the cathedral-like library. He knew her favorite spot, under the Venetian glass window, depicting the first woman receiving her degree in 15th Century Florence.

Susan's heart contracted when she sensed him behind her. He never wore cologne, but she knew the scent of his soap. He sat beside her and said nothing for a moment or two, fixing her with a serious gaze that caused her tummy to fill with butterflies.

"Gather up your books, we're going for a walk," he told her.

A light snow was beginning to fall as they followed the path beside the brook. Anthony stopped as soon as they were alone in the woods and picked up a fallen branch. Susan watched with great surprise as he broke off its longest, thinnest branch and swished it through the air with a whooshing sound. He looked at her without smiling.

"What are you going to do?" she backed away but he reached out and grabbed her by the wrist, then pulled her towards him and tucked her under his left arm.

"Teach you a lesson," he replied, bringing the switch down smartly on the seat of her dark blue jeans. Susan cried out with pain and surprise. The switch hurt! He held her fast. "Don't you dare move," he told her, "and be grateful I'm not taking your pants down for this!" He applied the switch to the backs of her calves now and she sobbed at the effect. Once more he switched her bottom, then her thighs, then her calves. She caught her breath and sobbed at each cut, but did not struggle to get away. Then came six hard strokes in a row, all across her bottom at evenly spaced latitudes. These cuts brought tears to Susan's eyes.

Anthony let her go. They sank down on the bank of the stream. She wept against his jacket while he held her.

"You let me down, Susan," he told her. "We've been together almost three years now and I've never known you to behave as immaturely as you have this week."

Susan hung her head, which looked particularly sweet in a heather wool beret, which was now becoming flecked with snowflakes.

"I expect you to be self reliant and resourceful when I can't be with you."

"I'm sorry," she accepted his handkerchief.

They walked back to the dorm called Main where Susan lived.

This was the original building of the college and it dated back to the Civil War. It was a grand, imposing winged edifice, fashioned after the Tuileries in Paris. Susan had a room in one of the fifth floor towers. She took him there.

It was a corner room with four windows, painted smoky blue with oak moldings. Her windows displayed autumnal vistas on every side. Anthony sat in one window seat and she in another while they speculated about the long history of the room they were in and the many women who had inhabited it.

"The first girl who lived here undoubtedly wore whalebone stays and had her own maid," Susan told Anthony.

"I wonder whether that young lady ever had marks to show her lover," Anthony mused. Susan took the hint and came to him. She allowed him to unzip her jeans, pull them down and then her panties. He laid her across one knee and caressed her bare bottom, which bore several traces of the switch. She was only lightly marked. It was enough to keep the glow of this afternoon alive until he returned.

Anthony locked the door and made Susan get on her little school bed, on her hands and knees with her bottom toward him. He penetrated her quickly and smoothly from behind, fastened his hands to her small waist and began to fuck her soundly. Anthony was young enough to have enjoyed the first wave of totally permissive college campuses, with coed dorms already established at Yale when he was an undergraduate. So he thought nothing of taking his girlfriend right in her dorm room. In spite of this room's pristine innocence for the first 100 years of its existence, the last 30 had been filled with scenes like this one. An elegant hotel would have been more to his taste, but he had no time to stay the night in the Hudson Valley and hadn't come to see her just to chastise her.

He admired the curvaceous symmetry of her bare bottom between his hands as he held by the hips and drove into her creamy pussy.

"I'm bringing home a cane from England, to replace the one you put in the incinerator," he warned her.

"But you said they don't make them anymore," she turned her head and caught their reflection in the mirror over her little oak dresser.

"Don't worry, I'll find one," he promised, tracing one of the light red marks left by the switch with a fingertip.

Susan closed her eyes and pushed back against him, returning each thrust as firmly as it was given. She went into a dreamlike state of endless pleasure whenever he took her like this. Sometimes the force of a thrust would remind her so much of a slap, or the stroke of a belt, that she would feel a deep, delirious contraction in her tummy. His forceful style conformed exactly to her needs. When she had sex, she wanted to be taken, just like this. She wanted it to be almost another act of discipline, and most importantly, an expression of control.

Anthony came before her, in the usual way, outside, not inside her lovely young body. Then he laid her across his lap and forced her to have an orgasm by digitally penetrating her bottom. It didn't take very long.

Soon after that he was putting his overcoat and hat back on and preparing to depart. Susan insisted on walking him downstairs. Dennis sprang out of the Bentley to open the door for his employer and greet Susan, who favored him with an affectionate smile before being swept into her lover's arms for one final kiss.

Susan rushed back to her room, remembering as she raced up the five flights of steps, how nimbly he had taken them beside her an hour before. After locking the door she examined her marks in the mirror. They were light for the pain she had felt. Although she didn't resent the switching, Susan inwardly resolved never to earn such a punishment again. Yet his strictness seemed very sexy in retrospect.

After Anthony forbid her to write him long letters and embarrassed her about writing to Dennis she had to find another worthy correspondent and she picked Michael Flagg. This choice was made in the spirit of sheer mischief, Susan deciding that she could not put off the pleasure of giving herself to the good looking detective any longer.

Michael received the first letter a few days before Thanksgiving, and it was Hugo who forwarded the letter to Michael from Susan. He opened it very late one night, after coming home from his shift. It was written in precise script, on one thick, perfumed sheet of cream stationary with the initials SR embossed on the top.

"Dear Michael," it began, *"I hope you will remember meeting me at the impromptu auto-de-fe which Hugo Sands arranged for the betterment of my sister Laura at the beginning of September.*

I am writing to let you know how impressed I was by your restraint that evening. You alone resisted the invitation to thrash Laura, even though she would have submitted, because you instinctively felt that it was not respectful to do so. Laura and I discussed it afterwards and she also appreciated your highly developed sense of propriety. (Which I hope you will completely ignore when dealing with me.)

I enjoyed it very much when you held my hand. Why did you do that?

Best Regards,
Susan Ross"

Michael's reply showed up in her mail slot the day before she left for Thanksgiving. She had it to look at in the back of the Bentley as Dennis drove her to Random Point for the holiday. She didn't even open the plain blue envelope until they were driving out of the grand, circular driveway fronting the entrance to her dorm. It began to rain as they passed through the main gate and Susan looked forward to enjoying the long drive to Massachusetts in the rain. Dennis was blissful up front, knowing he would get to talk to Susan when they stopped for a couple of meals and would be staying on the Cape the entire long weekend with Susan and her sister Laura, so he could be at her disposal and drive her back to college on Sunday night. She would be getting her license shortly and this would be the last time he would drive her to and from school.

Now Susan opened her letter and read the following lines, which were boldly scrawled on white letterhead.

Dear Susan,

Thank you for your letter. You are a thoughtful and adorable young lady, whom I would enjoy getting to know better when the time is right.

When I took your hand I hoped to distract you. You seemed disturbed by your sister's punishment. When I took your hand I forgot all about your sister.

Please feel free to call me if you'd ever care to chat at the phone number above.

Fondest regards,
Michael Flagg

Susan read the letter until she'd memorized it. Then she tried to figure out what to do next. Did she really dare to call him? Call him and chat about what? She revolved a number of scenarios in her mind and fell asleep dreaming about being in the power of Detective Flagg.

The next morning in Random Point dawned frosty cold. Susan and Laura put the turkey in the oven as soon as they could, then dressed in warm leggings and sweaters and went skating on the duck pond. Susan's heart began to pound fiercely as they glimpsed Michael Flagg already skating when they arrived.

Susan had already told Laura of her brief correspondence with Michael and had found her sister extremely sympathetic. When Michael skated over to them Laura invited him over for a turkey dinner later in the day. Gratified and slightly embarrassed by the soft attentions paid to him by the pretty sisters, Michael flushed but accepted the invitation, intending to visit the girls before beginning his shift at five.

Dennis, who was helping in the kitchen, suffered keenly at Susan's excitement over their tall, handsome guest.

Over dinner Susan and Laura begged Michael to tell them lurid police stories, which he obliged them by doing. Then it was time for him to go. Both girls insisted on kissing his cheek. He slipped his arm around Susan's small waist and gave it a firm squeeze. Their blue eyes locked when he let her go. He smiled at her, but Susan couldn't tell whether she was being encouraged or merely treated politely.

"Walk him to his car," Laura whispered. But Susan couldn't bring herself to do that, not knowing what to say.

She returned to school on Sunday night having gotten no further with Michael and unsure of how to proceed. Then on Monday afternoon she was surprised by an autumn bouquet, which had been left outside her door by a florist with a note from Michael, thanking her for the dinner. Laura also got flowers. He had also had written on the card to Susan, "I'd love to see some of your artwork and stories sometime."

Susan immediately went to the library and photocopied a comic strip she was working on and mailed it to him with a letter describing the week before her. It was the beginning of a correspondence that was characterized by long, sometimes illustrated letters from Susan and replied to in a friendly but circumspect style by Michael.

After about three weeks of polite and pleasant letters back and forth, Susan decided it was time to get a rise out of him. So she wrote a long and colorful letter about a recent jaunt to West Point she had made with a carful of rowdy seniors, drinking all the way there, then picking out cadets to engage with on Flirtation Walk. Susan casually bragged about a 6'6", buzz cut blond god managing to pull out and shoot with her just like a porno star after both of them drained his hip flask of JD in the bushes. It was enough. The letter she received back was brief and to the point.

"Dear Susan," it read, *"Remember I mentioned I have a wood-shed? One more letter like your last and you'll get to see it next time you're in Random Point.*

Michael"

Excited by the note, Susan finally decided to initiate the next phase of their affair. She'd stayed up late on whites editing the final draft of a paper that was due the next day and now intended to reward herself. Michael was on graveyard shift at the station when she called.

"Detective," he said, answering the phone, in a three a.m. voice that sent a shiver down her spine.

"Michael? This is Susan Ross," she said, thrilling to the sight of fresh snow falling against the black sky outside her window.

"Well, hello young lady. What are you doing up so late?"

"I just finished a paper and I was wondering..."

"Yes?" he leaned back in his chair with a smile. It had been snowing outside his windows for some time.

"Whether I'd get to see your woodshed when I come home for

Christmas."

"Now, Susan," he said, in a maturely discouraging tone, "the letters and the flirting have been charming, but realistically, aren't you spoken for?"

"Anthony doesn't have to know," Susan said quickly and without a twinge of conscience.

"I see," he replied noncommittally.

"You sound hesitant," she felt her heart contract with disappointment at his lack of enthusiasm for playing with her. "I probably shouldn't have called you so late."

"That's all right."

"Do you not want me to write you anymore?" she asked.

"I didn't say that."

"Are you afraid of falling in love with me?"

Michael laughed at her audacity.

"Very well, young lady," he told her, giving up his feeble attempt at circumspection, "we have an appointment the next time you're in Random Point."

"In your woodshed?"

"If you have the nerve."

"Oh, I do."

For the next week Susan fantasized about Michael Flagg continuously. In her studio art class she worked on a clay bust of his head, falling deeply in love with her creation and longing to see and touch the strong, virile body that supported that noble dome. She intended to photograph the piece for her portfolio, then bring it home and present it to him the following week.

Luckily, Anthony Newton did not mean to join Susan at his house in Random Point until Christmas Eve, which was several days after Susan intended to arrive, and he therefore missed the entrance of Susan with the bust. This was fortuitous, as she had decided that her current infatuation with Michael Flagg was best kept from her lover.

As soon as she had a chance to bathe and change her clothes, Susan called the second number that Michael had given her, which was his home number. She got his message machine, which informed her that he would not be home until midnight. Susan left a message that she would be happy to meet him at midnight.

When Michael checked his machine at ten he was delighted at the sexy message little Susan had left him. He called Anthony Newton's house and she drowsily answered the phone.

"You feel asleep, didn't you?" he admonished her. "I should have known that little girls couldn't stay up until midnight."

"I can stay up as late as I like," Susan said defiantly.

"I'll pick you up as soon as I can," he told her and hung up.

When he arrived just after twelve he found her waiting for him dressed in a perfect tartan jumper over a cream wool turtle neck, cream cashmere argyle knee sox and little mahogany oxfords. He had called her a little girl and she wanted to be that way for him.

It was snowing outside when she opened the door to him. Tall, fair and Viking like, Michael seemed to fill the foyer. She blushed very deeply when he took off his topcoat, handed it to her and watched her as she hung it in the closet. She escorted him through the richly carpeted hall way to the downstairs drawing room and offered him his choice of nightcap. He selected Irish whiskey. She refrained from drinking but watched him shyly as he drained the shot glass.

"You must be tired after working all day," she ventured awkwardly.

"I was, until I got your message."

"I've been very forward, haven't I?" she ventured, daring to meet his eyes, but only momentarily. He was clearly amused by her shyness and confusion.

"You are bold on paper," he agreed.

"In reality too," she said bravely, while inwardly trembling at his height and apparent strength.

"That's right. You're the one who keeps cadets out past their curfew at West Point, fucking them in the bushes."

"Oh, I only said that to be sensational."

"You mean you didn't really do it?"

"I did it. But I only bragged about it to tease you."

"Susan, get your coat."

Susan got her navy reefer coat and tam and his coat out of the closet and they both bundled up. Before leaving she brought a box out of the bottom of the closet and had him help her put it on a table.

"I made something I want to show you," she said, opening the box, taking out straw and the lifting out the bust.

"You made a bust of Joel McCrea?" Michael asked, examining the finely turned head.

"No, it's you," she explained indignantly.

"Me?" Michael laughed.

"Of course it's you and I think it's an excellent likeness."

Michael studied the bust, feeling immensely flattered.

"I want you to have it," she told him.

"Thank you. I'm overwhelmed," he replied, putting it carefully back in the box. Susan glowed with pleasure at the way her surprise made him flush.

Within ten minutes he was letting her into his refinished rustic cottage in the woods skirting Random Point. She didn't take her coat off until he'd started a large, crackling fire in the main room, which was graced by an imposing stone fireplace. The storm was whipping up thick drifts of snow about the woods and village and Susan was glad to be cozy inside.

Michael brewed her tea on a hot grate built into the hearth. She sat on an upholstered stool by the fire and drank her tea, hoping he'd leave the woodshed for an evening in summer. He came up behind her and ruffled her soft, long, wavy blonde hair. She turned to find him kneeling beside her. Unable to resist, she placed a tiny, innocent kiss on his face. Michael kissed her back, but without innocence. The next thing she knew they were both on the floor in front of the fire, she in his arms.

But as he drew her against him his hand inevitably curved around the swell of her girlish bottom and the touch of his hand on this portion of her body electrified them both. Michael pulled away, then let her go.

"No," he said, "this is too easy."

She knew exactly what he meant and her heart began to pound.

"Luckily for you, snowdrifts piled up against the door preclude a trip to the woodshed tonight; however, there is still the matter of the letter to be dealt with... "

Michael got to his feet and pulled her up to hers, then took her by the hand and led her to his favorite heavy straight-backed chair, whereupon he sat down and turned her over his knee.

"You didn't think you were going to get out of this, did you?" he asked, smoothing down her skirt over her heavenly little bottom.

"For a minute I did," she confessed, then gnawed on her knuckle and waited. Michael paused to enjoy their reflection in a full-length mirror across the room. Susan looked so adorably worried.

"Now, Susan, you knew very well that if you teased me enough I would spank you."

Susan had no reply to this fact. He patted her bottom. She squirmed.

"I like this jumper," he told her, smoothing down the skirt again.

"It's my actual prep school uniform," she told him pertly, over her shoulder.

Just when Michael thought his cock couldn't get any harder and was threatening to burst his zipper, she said something like that. Michael brought his hand down on her bottom no harder, he thought, than a boarding school girl deserved, for a minute or two, to warm her up. Susan squirmed and kicked her little shoes, but made no outcry. However, the small, breathy noises she did produce were those of startled and embarrassed pleasure. His large hand coming down so firmly on her bottom caused thrilling sensations to ripple through Susan's tummy.

"One can only imagine the sort of mischief you got up to in this," he remarked, raising the skirt to her waist to expose her cream silk panties, which clung snugly to her perfect bottom.

"I fucked my boyfriend in it constantly when I was 14," she blithely revealed.

"You know, young lady," he told her between hard, admonishing spanks, "you have an unbecoming habit of boasting about your sexual experiences that I find objectionable in one so young."

A sound spanking followed, while Susan kicked and squirmed. He easily held her firmly in placed with one large hand on her waist.

"Hold still, young lady," he told her. "I'm going to teach you a lesson about being more circumspect around people you hardly know," he scolded, pausing to lean down and look at her face.

"Ouch," said Susan, looking at him with wide eyes.

"I'm afraid I'm going to have to pull your panties down," he told her, tucking his thumbs under the waistband and lowering the briefs to mid-thigh. Susan's smooth, round bottom was already dark pink from the spanking on her panties and charmingly radiant. He pressed his lips to her bottom several times, causing her to catch her breath with surprise and look back at him. "Beautiful," he briefly explained, giving her bottom a pat.

"I'm sorry I said controversial things," said Susan with trepidation, as he raised his hand to smack her bare bottom. The flesh of her cheeks had begun to mark dramatically, but in his rapture Michael chose to ignore this warning.

"You said vulgar things," he corrected her, spanking her hard. She cried out at every swat now that they had become more severe and tried to put her hand back to protect her bottom.

"Even D.H. Lawrence used the word fuck and cunt in his novels," Susan pointed out.

"Yes, but you'll note that he put them into the mouth of an uneducated games keeper, not Connie Chatterley's," Michael gained his point and finished the spanking.

Susan knew that it was one of the hardest spankings she had ever received, yet she was so aroused by being handled and controlled by Michael that she accepted it as though it had been a mild love spanking. She didn't even cry. Whereas if Anthony had spanked her that hard, she knew she would certainly cry, because he never spanked her that hard unless he was angry with her. But Michael seemed so affectionate and protective towards her and his penis was so hard the whole time that she couldn't help but feel deeply loved as he punished her. He didn't dispense many compliments, but the way he looked at her and held her communicated tender admiration.

Finally he allowed her to stand up and pull her panties back up. She turned her face away, feeling embarrassed. Then she went to the mirror to pull up her skirt and pull the panty legs to one side so she could examine the possible damage. Susan was shocked to note that her bottom had been stained dark purple highlighted by a latticework of black and blue marks. She had taken a hard spanking! How could he have spanked her hard enough to mark her like this without causing her to scream for mercy, she wondered, touching the tender flesh, which now began to feel quite sore, with a tentative finger tip. She rubbed her bottom ruefully.

"I guess I asked for it, but... " Susan set her panties back to rights and let her skirt drop. "... I sure am marked." She frowned in consternation, walking around the room, absently rubbing her bottom while examining small objects of decorative interest.

"Is this going to cause a problem?" he asked, following her, stopping her, pulling up her skirt and pulling aside her panties to examine the damage. She looked over her shoulder with him at her thoroughly marked bottom.

"Only if you don't immediately fu-- make love to me," she told him with an impudent smile.

Michael evaluated the marking in the distracted manner of a person who suddenly realizes he is guilty of a rash deed. The sight of her poor, belabored bottom, which had come to him so pristine and white, was confusing and very distressing. He had never marked anyone with his hand before. Indeed, the only marks he had ever left had been with a strap, and even then, they were lighter and less bruise like than these. Had he really bruised this darling little girl? He knelt behind her to press his lips to her poor, punished bottom. She reached back to take him by the hair as a child grabs the mane of a favorite big dog.

"Did you hear me?" she asked.

"I want to put something on your bottom immediately," he told her, getting to his feet and disappearing into another room. Susan beheld the marks with awe, thrilled that he had spanked her severely enough to leave her this memory of him, because by now she was extremely enamored of Michael Flagg.

Michael returned with a towel and some aloe cream. He sat on the sofa by the fireside and beckoned her to him. When she came he took her across his knee again, but this time to apply the healing ointment to her bottom. He pulled down her panties and began to massage the cream into her purpling buttocks deeply and gently, still trying to sort out his feelings about what he had done. He deeply regretted placing ugly marks on her flawless bottom. But he understood from Susan's words and gestures that she had no resentment of him. She was sophisticated enough to know that marks were an occasional liability of playing and that if a girl didn't want to have to conceal them from her lover, she shouldn't let very strong men with extra large hands spank her on the bare bottom. Never the less, he worried. He ought to have stopped spanking her sooner. And he ought not to have spanked her so hard. She had done nothing to merit this sort of discipline.

"Hey!" she protested, "I think this is making it hurt worse!"

"I'm going to give you this cream to take home," he told her, "and I want you to use it at least twice a day. It should help the marks to go down. Another thing you can do is coat the area with toothpaste for about twenty minutes. It draws the bruising to the surface of the skin and makes it fade faster."

"Toothpaste?"

"Yes, my ex-wife Damaris learned about that when she worked in the B&D club."

He let her up and she set her clothes to rights again.

"Maybe we should do the toothpaste now, when it'll do the most good," Michael decided, abandoning her to go in search of toothpaste.

"No!" said Susan, rubbing her bottom. He came back with the toothpaste and sat down again.

"Come on, we're going to give this a try," he told her, pulling her back down across his lap.

"No, this is silly!" she protested, trying to pulling her skirt back down. She wriggled on his lap and tried to get away but he held her fast.

"Don't be obstinate, Susan. This is for your own good."

"I don't want you to put toothpaste on my bottom. It sounds like some old wives tale!" she thrashed against his thighs, trying to break his hold on her. "Let me go!" she said in a tone so angry that he immediately complied.

Susan jumped off his lap and then retreated to the other side of the room. Now that the clear and present danger of the toothpaste humiliation had passed, Susan calmly confronted him. Everything had changed in an instant between them. It was unfortunate that when he wanted so badly to charm her, all that he seemed to be doing was blundering. Such a look of consternation came over his face at this thought that Susan couldn't help but laugh.

"It's all right," she reassured him. "I'm not mad at you, just don't mention toothpaste again."

Michael wasn't used to being scolded by a girl, especially one almost young enough to be his daughter, and was painfully aware the fact that he was no longer in control of the situation.

"Why are you so quiet?" she came to him and sat on his lap, placing her lips against his throat between collar and ear.

"I'm just wondering what to do with you," he tightened his arms around her tiny waist and inhaled the perfume of her hair and skin. Her body was softly compliant as she put her arms around his neck.

"Why don't you let nature point the way?" she asked, bouncing impertinently on his lap, which still concealed a lead pipe she could feel through the layers of clothes between them. Michael's self doubt did not interfere with his body's response to her dear proximity.

He carried her into his bedroom, deposited her on the big, four-poster bed, and began to undress. Susan kept her eyes on him but also slowly began to get out of her outfit. She paused now and then to examine her bottom in the mirror opposite the bed.

"I'm going to say I went skating and fell a lot," she decided. His clothes were off before hers and she made a gratifying fuss over his physique. By the time she had kissed and caressed all the handsome planes and contours of his gracefully chiseled torso, Michael's confidence began to return. Susan didn't tell him of her fetish for bodybuilders, but her knowledgeable admiration of his major muscle groups gave her secret away. She begged him to pose for her nude.

Michael made no promises but began to unbutton her white cotton blouse, the jumper already being tossed on the floor.

"How do you like being made love to best?" he asked her, pulling off her blouse and cupping in his hands her small, rounded bosom, which was perfectly presented in a cream lace front closure décolleté bra. He gently undid the clasp and freed her breasts, which he then caressed and kissed.

"Face down and from behind, with my tummy pressed against something I can grind on," she answered in all frankness.

"Sounds easy enough," Michael said, placing a large oblong bolster cushion in the center of the bed. "Straddle that," he told her.

"Now?"

"Just to get the feel of it," he said, helping her. She was now in her pale silk panties and knee sox. She sat on the bolster and leaned forward, jutting her bottom back towards him and hugging the hard pillow with her knees on either side of it.

"Perfect," she said, leaning forward so that her lower abdomen was pressed flat against the bolster, which was richly covered in forest green damask. He got behind her and made her lean forward completely until she was face down against the pillow.

"Head down and bottom up," he told her, helping to raise her hips. He separated her knees as far as they would go and also spread her bottom. Susan gave a little cry of surprise. Then he reached between her legs to separate her labia with careful fingers. As he touched her he felt how wet she was and this brought a smile to his lips. It was a small vindication for part of his behavior, yet every time he focused on her bottom and saw the dreadful marking he had put there, he inwardly shuddered.

"Now Susan," he said, carefully working one middle finger in and out of her velvet pussy, "we don't have to go all the way."

"Huh?" she mumbled.

"I mean, I can get you off just like this, you know."

"Mmmm, that sounds nice," she murmured, "but let's try it the normal way first, so we can come together."

Michael lubricated his painfully hard organ with her own copious juices and slowly began the immensely satisfying task of penetrating her. He was large, but gentle and adept. Having been married to a petite woman, Michael knew that the key to fully taking a girl of Susan's size was to do it by slow degrees.

Susan closed her eyes and hugged the bolster. This was so exciting. She'd dreamed about this. She relaxed and opened herself to him. She peeked out of the corner of her eye into the mirror opposite the bed and thrilled to the sight of this extremely handsome and muscular male, invested with the authority of the state of Massachusetts, with his large hands which had subdued and disciplined her fastened to her waist and his hips thrusting forward every time he plunged inside her to the hilt. How she longed to sculpt those rock hard abs and pecs! Michael noticed her soft smile in the mirror as she shyly watched him take her and fell deeply in love. He stroked her bottom firmly while he plunged repeatedly into her delicious little pussy.

Then Michael brushed her long blonde hair away from her right ear and took her earlobe firmly between his thumb and forefinger in the manner of a disciplinarian.

"Are you ever going to write me such a naughty letter again?" he pinched her velvety ear lobe just hard enough for her to realize that she was being scolded.

"No," she replied, experiencing a ripple through her tummy, which foreshadowed the climax, she had been teetering on ever since he'd achieved full and vigorous penetration. "I'll write a worse one next time!"

"Oh. I see," he let go of her ear and sharply slapped her thighs. Susan cried out in shock and pain but the sensation produced by the discipline was tremendous. She ground against the bolster when he resumed taking her forcefully and gave a little sob when she came. Michael withdrew within a split second of his own climax and ejaculated against her bottom cheeks that he himself had so sternly marked.

They stayed up most of the night talking, with her curled against him and his arms around her in the dark. He found out that Laura and Susan had different fathers, which explained why Susan was an heiress and Laura was not. Susan had had a strict, scary, dominating, older father, who had tyrannized over her until his demise when Susan was in her senior year at prep school.

Michael was surprised that for all of the terror he had inspired, that Susan's father had only spanked her a couple of times, between the ages of 3 and 6.

"What do you suppose he would have done had he discovered the many uses of your school jumper?" asked Michael.

"Given me a strapping for sure," she said immediately. "And he would have pulled me out of school."

"But he never did find out about anything you did, did he?"

"No. I was a good girl."

"You mean you were a clever girl."

Michael in his turn revealed that he used to receive regular and severe strappings throughout his childhood from his former marine, cop father, whom he still resented greatly. Then Susan and Michael both agreed that children oughtn't to be spanked, except very occasionally.

"However, had my daddy been handsome and loveable and young, I might have enjoyed being spanked by him. I might even have been naughty on purpose, to get the attention," she mused.

"But that wouldn't have been proper," Michael pointed out.

"Why not?"

"Because then it would have been eroticizing your relationship."

"But it wouldn't have been sex, just spanking."

"I'm just telling you what I think."

"Suppose you had a little girl of five, who consciously provoked you into spanking her, would you refuse to satisfy her harmless little need?"

"It depends on how naughty she was in trying to provoke me. She might succeed."

"Sometimes when I see the cute, young daddies come to visit their daughters at school I wonder whether any of them have ever spanked any of my classmates. They're not making daddies like they used to, you know. Some of them even look like you."

"Yuppie daddies don't spank their daughters and you know it," Michael smiled at her optimism.

Susan snuggled against him and fell fast asleep.

The next morning Susan asked Michael to go skating with her at the duck pond. He had to drive her back to Anthony Newton's house so that she could change into leggings and get her skates. Michael waited in the car, reading the paper while she rushed inside.

She encountered Dennis immediately as he was in the process to taking in the milk and paper.

"Hi, Dennis," she tossed off lightly as she started up the stairs.

"Mr. Newton got in last night," Dennis quickly revealed in a hushed tone, stopping Susan cold.

"He did?" A dart of anxiety pierced her heart as she looked up towards the second floor landing. "What time?"

"About two a.m."

"Did he ask where I was?"

"Of course."

"What did you say?"

"That I didn't know."

"What happened then?"

"He went to sleep."

"Is that what he's doing now?"

"Yes."

"Okay. Thanks, Dennis," she said, and tiptoed lightly up the stairs to her room, with a racing heart, wondering whether she should lie if she ran into him now, or try to create an alibi by calling certain friends in the village who could cover for her. With her pulse still pounding, she exchanged her jumper for a skating skirt, turtle neck, cropped jacket and tam, all in shades of winter white and cream wool. Her leggings were flesh colored and the skates which she carried were sparkling white. Meanwhile she wore little ivory lace up boots.

She ran back downstairs in a very few minutes, highly aware of the fact at that her lover was a very light sleeper. But mercifully she was allowed to escape without being apprehended. However, had she looked over her shoulder and up before getting into Michael's car she would have seen Anthony Newton on his bedroom balcony, very much awake at nine a.m. and not a little curious as to who Susan was rushing off with without even coming up to see him.

As soon as Susan drove away Anthony called William Random, who was immersed in his newspapers and coffee.

"William, does anyone you know around here drive a late model Olds, navy blue?"

"Michael Flagg has an Olds Cutlass that's dark blue."

"Is that so? Thank you, William," Anthony said, hanging up, all mysteries resolved.

Susan took her time in returning home, figuring she was in for it no matter what time she got back. By now Anthony would have called around to William's and Marguerite's looking for her to no avail. So Susan spent almost two hours skating at the pond with Michael, after which they went to the Bone and Feather for a large breakfast.

"Are you going to get in trouble with Anthony for this?" Michael asked her as she prepared to get out of his car in front of the Cliff House at one.

"Maybe just a little bit," she said, playing down her anxiety.

"Don't lie about the skating. He'll know where you got the marks and if you lie it'll make it worse."

"I won't lie," she promised.

Michael took her hand and kissed it.

"Susan, if you ever decide you need a new boyfriend, I want to be first on your list."

"Thank you, but Marguerite would beat the living daylights out of me."

Michael smiled and kissed her.

"Wait til you get my next letter," Susan teased, running her hand across the bar of lead which had sprouted in his trousers at her proximity.

"Susan, behave!"

Susan hugged him and got out of the car. Taking a deep breath she entered the house. No sooner had she quietly shut the door behind her than Anthony Newton appeared on the second floor landing to frown down at her.

"Susan, come up here, I want to talk to you," he told her and then returned to his rooms. She threw her hat, jacket and skates into the closet and proceeded upstairs in the short pleated skirt and turtleneck. Anthony was dressed in a salt and pepper Donegal tweed suit that was cut perfectly for his lithe, medium frame. He wore a white shirt, no tie and had his short, dark hair slicked back. He was clean shaven and meticulous in every aspect of his appearance. Anthony's dark, cynical eyes riveted her the instant she entered the room with the trepidation of a schoolgirl who has far outstayed her curfew.

"Well?" he said, folding his arms and looking her up and down, "What have you got to say for yourself, young lady?"

"I'm sorry I wasn't here when you got in last night, but you know I wasn't expecting you for a couple of days," she explained.

"Why didn't you come up this morning when you came back to change your clothes? Dennis told you I was here."

"I...wanted to go skating," she replied slowly, aware of how childish this sounded.

"I see. Well, that explains this morning. What about last night? Did you spend the night with Michael Flagg?"

"Yes, sir," Susan lowered her eyes, feeling her face grow very warm.

"And how did this happen to come about? I didn't even know you two knew each other beyond meeting that once at Hugo's at the end of the summer."

"I saw him on Thanksgiving," Susan admitted. "After that, we began corresponding."

"You have, have you?" Anthony said, with a tinge of irritation, uncertain that his toleration levels would stand a strain as great as Michael Flagg.

"Well I have to write to someone!" she protested.

"Letters are one thing, spending the night in another man's arms is quite another!" Anthony paced. Susan flushed with guilt and excitement. He seemed genuinely annoyed. If one had to put a word to it, he almost seemed jealous this time.

Anthony took up his usual position at the piano and began to play a moody, dissonant piece by Scriabin, while fixing Susan with an accusatory stare. She came over to the piano and looked contrite.

"You'd better be careful, little girl," he warned her.

"Why?"

"Two can play the same game, you know."

"What do you mean?"

"I mean that I might have other correspondents besides you as well."

"Do you?"

"What do you think?" Anthony wondered whether Susan had the

vaguest idea of the type of following a composer who had had three hit Broadway shows could possess.

"I don't know. Tell me," she asked, with a pounding heart.

"There is one particular girl I could become very fond of, if I allowed myself to," he admitted, paralyzing Susan with dread.

"A girl?"

"To be quite frank, I haven't met her yet," he revealed, "And I'm not going to, until she turns eighteen."

Anthony was gratified at Susan's stricken look.

"Why? How old is she now?"

"Seventeen and a half," he replied coolly. "Shall I tell you about her?"

Susan nodded.

"She's a senior at the Julliard School. A pianist. She's got a terrible crush on me. She's been writing me for two years now. I haven't encouraged her much, though I can't help but be interested in her career. She's sent me several tapes of herself playing my music and they're quite charming. I could easily patronize her. She's been begging me to come to her recitals for years but I've steadfastly refused until now. With the slightest encouragement she'll fall helplessly in love with me. Young girls are like that. They're not all sophisticated like you, Susan."

"So, are you going to encourage her?" Susan sat down beside him on the piano bench, her eyes on his fingers on the keys.

"What would you do in my position?"

"I don't know. Is she pretty?"

"Would you like to see her photo?"

"Sure," Susan said, almost dizzy with fear. Anthony went to a secretary and came back with an 8" x 10" black and white head shot of a beautiful young lady with jet black hair, big, dark eyes, flawless skin, a bewitching mouth and a graceful nose. Susan stared at the photo a long time.

"Why haven't you met her before?" she asked, finally placing it on the piano.

"Because she adores me and she's still a minor."

"Noble of you," Susan said.

"Don't get smart. But do answer the question. What would you do about Elaine?"

"That's her name?"

"Elaine Ruskin."

"I guess that would depend on whether she was into d&s."

"D&S? Are you kidding? Who could possibly be more compliant than a protégé who is in love with her mentor? But beyond that, I do have one major proof of Elaine's potential as a future submissive. When she was fifteen she began sending me the most extravagant and fantastic letters I'd ever received. Even more shocking than yours. At the time I wrote her a brief note stating that she deserved a good spanking for spending more time writing to me than studying. Well, she never did stop writing me letters and every letter she has written since that date is signed with some reference to the day she can look forward to receiving that spanking from me."

Susan felt ill. She got up and paced. Anthony looked serious as he began playing again.

"So, what are you going to do?" she finally asked again.

"I don't know," he shrugged. "What would you do?"

"I wish you wouldn't keep asking me that."

"Why? Because you're a slut and the answer is obvious? As I said, Susan, two can play the same game." He got up and strode into his bedroom. Susan followed. When she did he grabbed her and threw her down on the bed.

"Come here, you little slut," he said, positioning her on her back. One by one he took her little feet between his hands and unlaced her boots to pull them off. His expression was neutral but his movements deliberate. She understood that she was about to be taken and not politely. He yanked down her leggings and then her beige stretch briefs and pulled them off. Susan's bare legs were very smooth and white and she had pretty, small feet.

"I'll teach you to run around with other men on the night before I get in!" he told her, spreading her legs and unzipping his trousers. He stopped to pull his jacket off and loosen his collar, then freed his large, fully erect penis. He inserted one finger deep into her blonde fuzzed public mound. She was lubricating nicely as he did this, suddenly very excited by the aggressiveness with which he had flung her on the bed and pulled up her skating skirt. "Who are you wet from, Susan?" he asked sarcastically, "the last one in or me?"

"You... I think," she answered, punishing his rudeness.

In a moment or two he was penetrating Susan forcefully, plunging in to the hilt with her bottom cheeks cupped in his hands. As he pulled her up and against him, one of his middle fingers found its way into her bottom. Susan wrapped her legs around his waist and pressed up against him until the tease became too intense to withstand and she climaxed. Anthony followed shortly thereafter, the spasms of her orgasm acting as a catalyst to his.

Susan escaped as soon as it was possible to do so and ran off to her room to lock herself in and change her clothes. As soon as he had stopped fucking her, the face of the girl in the photo came into her head and upset her. She exchanged the skating skirt and sweater for black pegged wool trousers, a grey linen shirt, black leather lug soled walking boots, a salt and pepper overcoat and a black suede cloche with gloves to match. Now that she looked more like a proper art major than a snow bunny she felt there would be less chance of people throwing her down on their beds and taking her without preamble. She headed immediately downstairs and out the door to begin a 2 hour stroll down the hill to the beach and then to Random Point.

She really had to think, though it twisted her heart to do so. Elaine Ruskin. She had looked like the young Natalie Wood. And a musical prodigy, who had adored him for years. Not yet 18! Susan felt so old at almost 21.

As she trudged down the hill, digging her little shoes into the melting snow on the gravel drive, she didn't hear Anthony come up behind her until he was at her side and this made her jump.

"Oh!" she cried.

"It's just me," he fell into step beside her, in a thick tweed overcoat and grey fedora. They walked for a few minutes without talking, enjoying the sharp, fresh, ocean air and flawless blue sky.

"Why are you so quiet?" he asked when they finally reached the rocky beach at the bottom of the cliff. "Feeling guilty about spending the night with Michael?"

"Not really," she admitted; "I was thinking about the girl."

"The girl?" he sounded puzzled.

"Elaine."

"Oh!" he smiled. "Don't worry about her."

"But everything you told me makes her sound exquisitely desirable."

"Almost like a fantasy come true?"

"Exactly."

"Elaine Ruskin is a character in a play I'm working on. The photograph is of the actress we're considering for the lead."

Susan felt her face grow very warm at this admission and she experienced one of her rare moments of anger.

"You were playing with me then?"

"Just teaching you a lesson," he replied matter of factly. They began to walk again, she trying hard to conquer her impulse to tell him off. He glanced at her to try to gauge her mood but she refused to look at him for the next hour.

They walked down into the town and Anthony told her he wanted her help with his Christmas shopping. This obviated the need for any significant conversation between them for the next several hours. By the time Anthony called the house to have Dennis pick them up he had all but forgotten the events of the morning, having spread much good cheer in the village and been fortified by strong mulled cider. But Susan hadn't forgotten and she returned to brooding as soon as they got home. Anthony noticed and pulled her into the music room as soon as she hung up her coat.

"What's going on?"

"You shouldn't have told me that horrible lie," she accused, on the verge of tears.

"Why not?"

"It upset me."

"Oh! And you don't think it upsets me to find out you're conducting intimate correspondences with other men? And then fucking them?"

"But -"

"Yes?"

Susan hung her head.

"You should be down on your knees begging my forgiveness for the disrespect you've shown me. Instead you're sulking because of a mild reproof."

"Mild reproof? You told me that story to make me violently jealous!"

"And did it?"

"It made me ill."

"Then you'd better mind your manners with me," he told her coolly. Susan felt a dart through her stomach as she dared to meet his eyes. If there was one thing which Susan could not resist, it was a handsome man who chose to affect a stern demeanor.

"I'm not sure I understand what that means," she said.

"It means that if you keep on having affairs with other men I'm going to start having affairs with other women and there won't be any point to our cohabitation."

"But I haven't been having affairs," she protested, frightened at the finality of his statement. "I've just been getting into a little mischief now and then."

"A bit too close to home, young lady."

Susan couldn't decide whether he was really angry with her or still just trying to teach her a lesson.

"May I be excused?" she asked politely. He allowed her to leave and immediately sat down at the piano, wondering whether he'd been too harsh with her. The cohabitation line had made her tremble and he knew that she had been on the verge of tears when she left. But damn it, he thought, beginning a vigorous Rachmaninoff prelude, she had to be taught not to take him for granted.

Then he suddenly remembered how roughly and crudely he had taken her directly she came home after being with Flagg and inwardly winced. "Did I do that?" He stopped playing, got up and paced. Perhaps her feelings had been hurt by that unromantic assault. He decided to go to her room.

He knocked and found Susan curled up in her window seat, looking out at the darkening sky as it was almost evening now.

"Susan?" he went to her and sat beside her and took her hand.

"What are you doing?"

"Nothing," she replied, tears ready to fall.

"I'm sorry I was mean to you just now," he told her, kissing her hand.

"You don't love me anymore," she declared and started to cry.

"Susan, how can you say that?" he pulled her into his arms. She felt very warm against him, almost feverish. The dampness of her soft white skin against his shirt front and the smell of her hair aroused him greatly. "You know you're the love of my life," he said sincerely.

"I am?" she raised her eyes to his.

"Of course you are."

"No," she pulled away, jumped up, walked away, then shyly looked at him. "You don't love me anymore."

"Now, why do you say that?"

"Because you didn't... "

"Didn't what?"

"You didn't spank me when you found out I spent the night with Michael."

Anthony found it difficult not to smile at this complaint,

"I see," he replied, considering what he should do.

"I suppose I'm very simple," she said, not meeting his eyes.

"You're very naughty. Susan, come over here."

Susan went to him and he pulled her down across his lap. A breathless "Oh!" escaped her lips as she was put in this position, with her woolen trousered bottom upturned for his hand. He fastened one hand on her waist while raising the other and soon he began to bring it down, with extreme determination, on the seat of her pants. Susan was thrilled to be pulled across his lap and spontaneously spanked over her clothes. After a volley of ten smacks he stayed his hand on her bottom. She realized she'd been gasping with excitement during the last few spanks and had also begun to grind against his muscular thighs. He found this very endearing and gave her a good rub, which made her grind even harder.

"Stand up," he told her, helping her to her feet, then unbuckling her belt and pulling down her zipper. Next he yanked her pants down to mid-thigh and put her back across his lap. Her sand colored French cut cotton briefs hugged the round cheeks of her small bottom tightly. Anthony brought the palm of his hand down vigorously ten more times on the voluptuous little seat of her panties. Again the swift volley of hard smacks took her breath away and freshets of lubrication dampened her panties. Once again he paused, this time to pull her panties down, which immediately revealed the particulars of how she had spent her evening with Michael Flagg.

"Susan, you're terribly marked," he told her, running his palm across her black and blue mottled cheeks with care. "What in the world was Michael thinking of?" The marking had already begun to fade considerably since the previous night, but the bruising was still shocking.

"It didn't seem that hard at the time," she said over her shoulder.

"You know what? I just remembered something. Get up," he tumbled her off his lap and strode into her adjoining bathroom.

"What?" she began to pull her panties back up, sorry that the spanking was over.

"Toothpaste reduces bruising!" he announced, coming back with a tube of toothpaste. Susan sighed and stretched out face down on the bed.

Chapter Four

Michael and Patricia

Patricia Fairservis, 32, divinely fair, slim and expensively dressed, entered the taproom of the Bone and Feather Inn on an oddly balmy December afternoon and scanned the booths for the sight of a man in a khaki poplin suit with a pink carnation in his buttonhole.

The editor of Cape Cod Style had pinned a white flower to the lapel of her own faultlessly tailored grey wool suit. Patricia paused before the mirror, lit a cigarette and scrutinized her straight, shiny, shoulder length honey blonde hair for imperfections, before allowing her gaze to rest upon the man.

"Michael F. or Code 8C?" she referred to the designation of his personal ad. He rose and shook her beautifully manicured hand.

"Hello, Patricia," replied Michael Flagg. He possessed two short, exciting, well written letters from this woman. She'd let him know immediately that she was a very bad girl. He knew she'd be pretty, but he hadn't been expecting someone quite so gemlike.

"Well, you're an unexpected surprise," she frankly observed, though not without a blush, sliding into the booth opposite him. If he was half the ripped hunk he looked, Patricia anticipating spending the night in the charming village of Random Point, Massachusetts.

He smiled and echoed her remark, "I can't understand why you refused to exchange photos."

"I never exchange photos," Patricia revealed, requesting the wine list from the young Inn Keeper, Connie Barton.

"Why is that?" Michael asked.

"As I wrote you, I'm married, but my husband is unaware of my activities. I'd hate for a disgruntled playmate to embarrass me."

"Do you answer many ads?"

"I meet a new person about twice a month," she coolly admitted, then added to herself with absolute candor, 'But never one who belonged on the cover of a bodice ripper!'

"Tell me all about your experiences with the ads," Michael said, lighting her newest cigarette.

"Well, I've only been playing for about six months, and it's been thrilling, in its way, but so far I haven't met a man I liked enough to have an affair with."

"You must have stringent requirements if you've managed to remain pure for 6 months," Michael observed.

"I didn't say I remained pure," she hastened to declare flirtatiously, "I only meant I haven't gone back for seconds so far." She then turned to Connie to order a very expensive bottle of wine, after which she presented the Inn Keeper with her card and promised to confer with her that evening about profiling the hostelry in an upcoming issue of her magazine. Michael was favorably struck by her sweetness of manner towards Connie, which indicated a pleasant disposition.

"What about you, Michael? Are you what they call an experienced player?"

"If I have any experience at all it's only due to my dumb luck in picking Random Point to move to."

"Oh? Why is that?"

"An abnormally high concentration of women in the scene live around here."

"You're married, though, right?" she asked, tasting and accepting the wine when it arrived.

"As I stated in my ad, I'm separated and seeking a compatible playmate."

"How long have you been separated?"

"Almost 4 months."

"And why did your wife leave you?"

"That would be telling. But how did you know that she was the one who left me?"

"I just knew. It wasn't because you... spanked her, was it?" asked Patricia in a hushed tone. Michael smiled and shook his head.

"When you say compatible, what exactly do you mean?" she asked, draining her first glass of wine.

"Well, obviously, my companion would have to enjoy discipline, as I think you do... ?"

"I think I do also, but I'm not sure," she said; "I don't necessarily want to be punished. I merely want to feel punished," explained Patricia with care. Thick, sandy lashes fringed her blue eyes, which fixed him with a thoughtful gaze.

"I understand," said Michael. She seemed touchingly new to this and he suspected her tolerance for spanking was that of a child.

"I've met with a couple of men who misunderstood what I wanted and hurt me."

"Tell me where they live and I'll kill them."

"Thank you!"

A pleasant lunch was passed in this manner, with Michael and Patricia mildly flirting while he decided what he was going to do with her and she waited in a torment of anxiety for him to do it.

Agreeing to drive the short distance to his house in the woods, they rose to depart. At this point a small incident occurred which signaled an end to the perfect harmony which had graced the first hour of their relationship.

When Flagg asked Connie to put the bill on his tab, she informed them that the lunch and wine were presented to Mrs. Fairservis and guest, compliments of the inn. Patricia, who of course, expected this courtesy, as the editor of Cape Cod Style, was never the less relieved, in view of the dearness of the wine. But she was annoyed when Michael failed to leave a proper gratuity.

"Would you mind?" she asked.

"Mind?"

"Leaving the tip?"

"Oh, sure," he said and placed a five on the table.

"Could we possibly do a little better than that, sweetheart? We just consumed a $65 bottle of wine," said she, stunning Flagg.

"Don't worry about it," he told her, steering her away from the table by the elbow. "Connie will get her plug, after all. You just told her so."

"Still!" Patricia insisted, dug in her Chanel purse and added another twenty dollar bill to the table before allowing him to lead her away. "I despise parsimony," she advised him as he handed her into the driver's seat of her late model Mercedes convertible.

"I can see that," he observed, taking in every gleaming inch of the smoky blue Germanic wonder and praying to the god he didn't believe in never to make him responsible for this woman's charge card bills. "But, sweetheart," he echoed her facile endearment with amusement, "do you really think you're fit to drive after all that wine?"

"Piece of cake," she assured him, pulling smoothly away from the curb.

He directed her to his house, via a bumpy, narrow woodland road, which the precision car rolled over smartly. At this point she pulled out the fattest joint he had ever seen and asked him if he minded if she got high.

"Not at all!" Michael was cheerfully encouraging.

"So, what do you do for a living?" she asked, casually exhaling pungent billows of smoke.

"I'm a cop," he replied, amused by the stricken look this confession inspired, until the distracted Patricia almost drove off the road.

"Maybe you'd better let me drive," he told her. She stopped the car without arguing and they switched seats. "I always wanted to drive one of these," he revealed happily. She stared at him. He patted her knee.

"It's okay," he told her, "I've never busted a girl I wanted date."

"Is that what you want to do?"

"Sure, my favorite hobby is trying to straighten out co-dependent submissives."

"Really? What's your success rate?"

"Zero," he said, parking in front of the cottage.

Patricia was impressed by Michael's beautifully redone turn of the century cottage, with its lavish wood paneling and ingenious built-ins.

"Want to buy it? You need a getaway house, Patricia," Michael suggested vigorously.

"Why would you want to sell it?"

"The payments are heavy for one person."

"You may marry again."

"I don't think so. Marriage is too restrictive."

"Now I understand," Patricia admired a beautifully framed portrait of Damaris which adorned the mantelpiece. "You were unfaithful to her once too often and she left you, right?"

Michael was amused by his sophisticated new friend. She was irritating, but likable and smart. She was also physically very appealing to him and this enhanced their first moments alone. To the limited extent that a sensible man can entertain such a notion, Michael realized that he was already in love with her.

Since Patricia was in the scene, he showed her his playroom.

"You'd be hard put to describe the uses of some of these furnishings to your readers," Michael pointed out, pulling down from a mahogany wall cabinet a spanking bench of upholstered leather, scooped in the center and the perfect height to bend a girl over. A set of leather straps were attached to hold the culprit in position.

Patricia blushed deeply as she regarded this custom built piece of equipment and was about to nervously stroll away from its proximity when Michael reached out and grasped her wrist.

"Try it," he told her, gently pushing her down across the saddle before she had a moment to protest. She noticed a mirror opposite as she went over, in which she was now able to observe the entire tableaux of which she was the focus.

Michael placed one hand on the small of her back to hold her in place then smoothed her skirt down over her trim, shapely bottom. She looked back at him.

"Perhaps this is a bit esoteric for starters," she suddenly suggested, popping up off the bench in a sprightly manner. She had either become embarrassed or taken a sudden fright, but the opportunity to utilize the spanking bench seemed to instantly pass. He folded his arms and fixed her with a look that made her tummy spasm.

"This is a bit fancy," he agreed, "when what you really deserve is a just a good, old fashioned, spanking," he told her, removing his jacket.

"But, why?"

"For making that scene about the tip at Connie's."

"But you were wrong!" asserted Patricia, stamping one small foot, which was shod in a pump costing more than a used car salesman earns in a month.

"I was not wrong, you snotty brat. I just happen to be aware of the fact that one doesn't tip the innkeeper."

"If one is a cheapskate one seizes upon every available loophole to avoid rewarding those providing goods and services," she pointed out. A champion of waitresses, shop girls and cab drivers was Patricia.

"That's your point of view, is it?"

"Your own profession, for example, is notorious for perquisite abuse, isn't it?" charged she triumphantly, slipping momentarily out of grabbing range.

"I really wouldn't know," he told her, clearly not amused. Her heart began to pound but she lit a cigarette.

"Come on, give me a break," she replied.

"Patricia, am I going to have to give you a lesson in manners so soon?"

"I suppose that's entirely up to you," Patricia ventured with a blush.

"You are a little monster," he told her. "But I think that you might benefit from correction."

"Correction from you?" said Patricia, daring to raise her eyes to the stranger who was about to become her best friend.

"I think it's the only possible way for me to address your behavior today at the Inn."

Michael strode across the room, took the cigarette away from her and took her by the arm. "Come over here, young lady," he told her, within inches of his favorite straight backed chair.

Michael noticed that she offered no resistance as he turned her over his knee and adjusted her to his satisfaction. She was very light across his lap and the tight suit skirt encased her bottom provocatively. She looked back at him and said, "Oh dear, are you really going to do this?"

Michael did not smile when he replied, "I'm afraid you need it."

Patricia dropped her head and waited, her stomach full of butterflies.

"Patricia?" he paused with his large hand resting on the curve of her girlish bottom.

"Yes?" she replied, turning her head slightly towards him.

"Do you need to be treated like a naughty little girl?"

"Yes!" she replied, dropping her head, with a tiny sob of emotion; her answer caused him to immediately tighten his grip on her waist.

"I think you need a spanking," he told her, patting her bottom lightly, then more firmly. She wriggled on his lap, still tightly wrapped in the tailored wool suit.

Then Michael began to spank this sexy, savvy, important woman just as though she were a child of six.

He administered a thorough spanking over her skirt, firmly alternating cheeks, with heavy, determined strokes of his large right hand while he held her in place with the left. Now and then the smacking caused her to kick up her heels but she made no serious attempt to escape. Each slap which fell upon her bottom sent a thrill through her slender frame and caused her sex to throb. The rock hard penis shape which she felt through both their clothes, seemed agreeably large.

Then she was suddenly set on her feet.

"Now let that be a lesson to you," he told her sternly. Patricia melted and was speechless. She would have followed him to hell. Sensing his advantage he pulled her towards him and began to undress her. She stood still, kept quiet and let him. Patricia didn't even dare meet his eyes. She was embarrassed and afraid she might laugh.

Presently, he bent her over the spanking bench and took her from behind. Patricia couldn't resist staring in the mirror throughout this performance, particularly when he fastened his hands to her waist and drove into her like John Leslie. He even pulled out at the last moment, as an adult performer would and delivered his copious benediction all over her bare, upturned, bottom.

However, the first thing Patricia did when she regained her footing was to deal him a resounding slap across the face.

"How dare you fuck me without protection?" she charged furiously. Now it was Michael's turn to flush as only a person of Celtic ancestry can.

"I'm sorry," he stammered, sincerely.

"Oh, never mind, I'm sure you're safe." Patricia felt a pang of guilt at the red imprint of her palm on Michael's face. "I'm sorry," she kissed his face and nuzzled it.

"No," he locked his arms around her waist. "I had it coming. And I think you're wonderful."

Much later that night, after completing his shift, Michael came to Patricia's room at the inn and she opened the door to him half drowsy, in a sleeveless surplice gown of white silk.

"Is it too late to come in?" he whispered, embracing her briefly in the doorway in defiance of all convention. She drew him inside and locked the door at once.

"Get back in bed," he ordered as it seemed chilly in the room. "Your fire's almost cold," he observed and hastened to load on logs. Patricia got back under the down comforter and gazed upon the tall, fair haired man removing his jacket and placing his valuables on the antique marble dresser top. The sight of his service revolver in its holster excited her.

"Michael, is it true that cops have groupies?" she asked, holding the coverlet up to her chin until the fire began to blaze.

"Only the ones who give out drugs." He sat on the bed beside her.

"Will you give me drugs from now on?"

"No."

"Will you come and visit me in Boston?"

"Just tell me when," he told her, pulling the top of her gown open and covering her satiny bosom with his hands. Her breasts were elegant and perfect, neither large nor small but voluptuously round and firmly upstanding.

"Michael," said Patricia, "do you see that charming little sofa by the fire? I chose this room because of it."

Michael appreciated her directness. For a spoiled brat she was thoughtful. He carried her to the sofa to administer that perfect spanking by the fireside which she had envisioned when the Innkeeper Connie had shown her the room that afternoon.

After warming the seat of her silk gown for several minutes,

Michael lifted the hem and bared her flawless bottom for a protracted spanking interspersed with deep caresses and a thorough finger fucking that left her soaking wet.

After the spanking, which lasted a long time and during which Patricia had her first climax ever while over the knee, they went to bed and made love.

The next day Michael began a week's vacation by driving Patricia back to Boston. They were already in love and both of them knew it. But Michael was also in love with two other women and this presented certain problems.

The first thing Patricia did when they got to Boston, after a devastatingly romantic drive, during which they had stopped several times in the woods to play, was to present Michael Flagg to her husband, Lawrence Fairservis, a Harvard professor, with whom she shared a Back Bay triple-decker. She introduced Flagg as the home security expert whom she'd engaged to make the building burglar proof, a sudden inspiration, as it would mean that Michael would have a legitimate reason to visit the house more than once that winter to figure out and install a system. Patricia's husband was a large, cheerful, robust man who was highly social and enjoyed dining out. He delivered all of Patricia's important messages succinctly, made a few cynical comments about mutual friends and actually gave his wife's bottom an affectionate but meaningless pat through her cream cashmere sweater dress. He then shook Michael's hand, wished him luck, informed Patricia of a fund raiser dinner he was attending that evening and disappeared into his study.

"He's a nice man," Patricia told Michael, pulling the detective into her private dressing room for a dangerous kiss.

Later that afternoon they strolled through Back Bay, stopping in little antique and art deco shops. Patricia insisted on buying him a clock for his mantelpiece at home in Random Point.

"So you'll know it if I'm late," she informed him with a mischievous smile. Michael felt a thrill at the implications of this simple statement but he was suddenly oppressed with musings which blunted his enjoyment of her enthusiasm. Noticing a change come over her new friend's face, Patricia asked him what the matter was. Michael simply shook his head and told her he had had enough of shopping for one day.

As they walked along the Charles, with the winter wind whipping their faces, Michael told Patricia about Damaris and Marguerite.

"They sound as if they're both too good for you," the blonde girl observed at length. "You'd better start dating me instead."

As Patricia's job took her up and down the Cape on an almost daily basis, it wasn't difficult to coordinate several meetings a week between Random Point and Boston. Patricia would always book them into the choicest bed and breakfasts and more often than not they stayed free, in return for the favorable review Patricia would then write.

Michael admired his new friend greatly, in spite of the fact that Patricia was a selfish girl. She wanted everything her way, at all times, and if she didn't get it, she threw tantrums from hell. She had no fear of Michael. She had no circumspection. He was used to women like Marguerite, Damaris, and Laura, who chose their words carefully, cultivated modest demeanors and let their eyes do the rest. Patricia said whatever came into her head. She was capable of the most insulting remarks and behavior. She was arrogant, opinionated and savagely jealous.

Their affair wasn't two weeks old before she began to give Michael ultimatums. He had to stop seeing Marguerite and trying to see his estranged wife. If he didn't do these two simple things she'd have to stop seeing him. She pointed out that there were multitudes of men in the scene she could date. Michael attempted to reason with her, encouraging her to date all the men she wanted, so long as she left time for him. This made her furious. Once she met Michael she had no further desire to date other men.

Accepting her faults, Michael rapidly became attached to Patricia. Her passion contented him much more than her possessiveness irritated him. It was refreshing to play with a woman who actually deserved to be spanked and spanked hard, at least once a day. The more he knew Patricia, the more he admired the subtle restraint of both his wife Damaris and his long time lover, Marguerite. These women left much unsaid. Even when they behaved in ways which could only be described as lifestyle radical, they never did so at the risk of that certain natural dignity which they both possessed. He recalled that the other two local girls in the scene he most admired, Laura Random and her sister, Susan Ross, were also exquisitely well behaved around men, except for exhibiting a bit of provocative rebellion now and then just to spark the interest. Patricia, on the other hand, embodied every negative female stereotype Michael had ever heard of, but had never encountered before, from PMS to maxed out charge cards. Every positive about her was cancelled by a resounding negative. Patricia was angelic to shop girls and waitresses, hellish to friends and loved ones. Patricia was one of the most feminine women he had ever met, possibly because of the shocking sums she spent on maintenance. You couldn't undress her without running into a Fernando Sanchez teddy in pure silk. Naturally he liked this, but it frightened him as he wondered who had the privilege of paying for all of this.

Patricia was fascinated by everything in Michael's life, his police work, the adventures he had had and all of his ambitions. However, the more she discovered about his former relationships, each of which appeared to be on-going, the less secure she felt.

In theory, Michael was ready to give everyone else up. Until he happened to run into Marguerite Alexander in the woods, striding along in a sweater and jeans with her long red hair down her back and the most ravishing color in her face. Nor could he help his heart from pounding uncontrollably whenever he encountered his wife in town. She made a point to avoid him whenever she could. When she did allow their eyes to meet, he felt almost physically ill at the thought of having lost her. At this point she wouldn't even favor him with a conversation beyond what was strictly necessary to tie up their affairs. She was divorcing him and he was not contesting it. Damaris was conducting herself with dignity and style. These were concepts alien to Patricia in all but matters of fashion and home decoration. That Damaris Perez Flagg should give up her magnificent, if somewhat unfaithful man so easily mystified Patricia. Particularly after the first time she beheld the Puerto Rican pocket Venus in the village while she was on the arm of Flagg. It was a horrible moment. Fortunately, for

Damaris, she was herself in the company of her employer, William Random. Both girls felt dizzy and ill upon confronting each other for the first time. Patricia was astonished that Michael should have allowed such a beauty to walk out on him and feared for their eminent reunion. Damaris saw a blue eyed blonde with her blonde blue eyed husband and thought how well they looked together. She appealed to William to take her away he was happy to oblige her. Patricia noticed the two men, who were friends, exchange rather helpless glances at the embarrassing situation before all four parted to go their separate ways.

That night Michael and Patricia had a dreadful fight about Damaris and the fact that he was still in love with her. But this was nothing compared with the explosion which came the first time Patricia glimpsed and spoke with Marguerite.

It was Patricia who insisted on visiting Marguerite Alexander's book shop. In the middle of the visit she was to figure out that the stunning proprietress with the Julie Newmar figure was Michael's other lover. Marguerite was all charm and friendliness to both of them, though a few slightly warmer words and glances tossed in Michael's direction were quite enough to clue Patricia in as to the redhead's relationship with the good looking detective.

Patricia was thrown into a turmoil of anguish and envy contemplating Flagg alone in the village five nights out of seven with those two sirens in the closest possible proximity. To make the situation even worse, Patricia actually happened to walk in on Michael while he was entertaining another neighborhood visitor, Laura Random, the estranged wife of William Random.

Laura had dropped into Michael's one Saturday afternoon solely to flirt. In the process of this enjoyable activity, Patricia arrived and had to be introduced. Laura had been flirting with Michael for several years and had planned to lay siege to him that winter. But Patricia made it abundantly clear that Michael was hers now. Laura sensed the force of Patricia's attachment and pleasantly slipped away to wait a while longer for the perfect scene with Michael which she had been fantasizing about ever since he had given her the little birthday spanking in Marguerite's shop years ago.

Meanwhile, Michael did his best to assuage Patricia's anxieties by courting her continuously all winter. At first he didn't know how to handle their quarrels. He attempted to console her, to appease her, to prove his love through as many hours of attentive devotion as he could offer in view of their separate commitments. But nothing ever seemed to soothe her. Nor could he appeal to her powers of reason, of which she seemed woefully bereft on the subject of love. Try as he might to point out that she herself was married and slept with another man at least sometimes, she would barely acknowledge the commitment. Her marriage didn't count in the equation because Lawrence wasn't in the scene and didn't turn her on.

Once, when Michael and Patricia were spending a weekend in New York so that she could review a small hotel, they were browsing in Saks Fifth Avenue and he was recognized by little Susan Ross, looking extremely cute in wool knickers and a sweater, who blushed deeply as they chatted. When Susan told Michael she'd be visiting Random Point over the weekend and that maybe she would run into him at the skating rink, Patricia's heart contracted. She couldn't leave the subject of Susan alone for the rest of the day.

Michael described the particulars of only his first meeting with Susan in the early autumn. He did not omit the fact that he had briefly held Susan's hand while they had watched Laura Random being cropped by Marguerite. These details caused Patricia to feel ill with jealousy. Hating herself for doing so, she accused Michael of wanting Susan.

"It's only a matter of time before you fuck her," declared Patricia as they strolled through Central Park on a cool winter afternoon. It was about 3pm and many of the beautiful, secluded walks were empty. "I just hope for your sake she's of age."

"Patricia, cut it out, I have no intention of fucking Susan Ross." ('At least until the next time I have the opportunity,' he added to himself.)

Patricia was of course very foolish to have worried about other women that day, as fetching as she looked in her buff leggings, heather beige tweed blazer and cream wool turtle neck. The little urban hiking boots, worn with rolled sox, allowed her to scramble up the hilly paths around the park with tomboyish grace. Her thick, glossy blonde hair hung to her shoulders in a Veronica Lake finger wave that kept him hard all afternoon.

Michael added, "You're horrible."

"It's no use," she informed him, turning abruptly, "I can't go on like this. You just have too many women. You don't need me."

"Patricia, as I've told you before, those girls are just friends in the scene. You're the one I'm interested in now," he took her by the shoulders and made her look at him.

"Until you go home to Random Point," she said resentfully.

"So leave your husband and move in with me," Michael suggested.

Patricia stared at him.

"You're just saying that because you know I can't do it," she finally decided.

"Why can't you?" They began to walk again.

"I need to be in Boston for the magazine. You know the social demands I'm subject to."

"You can live on the Cape," he told her.

Patricia was impressed by his offer, which left her speechless for several moments.

"Why do you have the need to going skating with that little girl?" Patricia suddenly demanded. Michael sighed.

"Patricia," he said quietly, "didn't I just invite you to live with me?"

"Yes."

"Then what's the problem?"

"I just don't think you ought to see other women."

"I'm not seeing other women. And I'm getting tired of telling you that. Come over here," Michael said, taking Patricia by the wrist and dragging her over to a bench.

"What are you doing? No!"

Michael turned her over his knee and spanked her hard. His large hand came down rapidly on her small, round, bottom, so snugly encased in the nubby woolen leggings. She kicked her legs but didn't try to get away.

"I'm going to cure you of this ridiculous jealousy," he promised, administering several dozen smacks.

"Oh, please, Michael, don't! What if someone comes?"

"Then someone will see you getting spanked," Michael finished with half a dozen extra hard slaps, then placed her on her feet. "Now let that be a lesson to you, young lady. From now on, every time you utter an irrationally jealous remark, I'm going to paddle your bottom. Do you understand?"

"No!"

"Really? Well, let me clarify my remarks," Michael told her, and once again sat down and pulled her across his lap. But this time, just as Patricia went over, a young couple, probably lawyers, came strolling into her view, he in a black cashmere overcoat and scarf, she in a smart grey wool suit, top coat and perfect boots. Both had white skin that never saw the sun except by accident and jet black hair. They looked at each other and smiled at the frivolous blonde children they'd stumbled onto playing spanking games in the park. Patricia was deeply humiliated and tried to jump off his lap but Michael held her fast and having ascertained that their visitors were not the type to interfere began to vigorously apply the palm of his hand to the seat of her pants as before, only more so. Patricia was speechless with indignation as Michael continued to spank her and she was forced to meet both the eyes of the girl and the man. They both seemed amused and joined hands before strolling out of sight.

"I'll scream if you don't let me go!" Patricia cried, imagining she saw a group of boys in plaid shirts and turned around baseball caps approaching through the trees. "I mean...what if some unsavory persons happened by when you were taking these sorts of liberties with me...!" she very sensibly appealed to his protective instinct.

"Oh very well," he said, letting her up and resuming their walk.

"We don't want to get me gang banged, right?" she rubbed her bottom with both hands as they walked along.

Michael could not fail to notice that she was good for the rest of the day. He then began to realize that Patricia needed to be civilized.

Their attachment for each other grew, exacerbated by the onset of Spring. Patricia's husband departed for a sabbatical in Italy, freeing her from her few domestic responsibilities for the remainder of the season. This new development naturally made Patricia more restless than ever while her longing for Detective Flagg increased.

Michael was perfectly ready to fall in love with Patricia. He enjoyed her sarcasm, even when he was the butt of it. Of course, he wasn't about to let Patricia know that. 95% of her insults Michael virtually ignored, while inwardly agreeing with her. Now and then, for the sake of his own dignity, and because she would have been disappointed otherwise, he felt compelled to punish her for her rudeness.

Patricia added a degree of glamour and excitement to his life which he allowed himself to enjoy without reserve. She also bothered to tempt him in ways which he found quite enchanting. With Damaris he was always the one to decide that they were going to play. With Marguerite he was lucky, very lucky, when he could get her to give in and play. But Patricia initiated encounters with a charming enthusiasm.

Once, for instance, when he arrived at her house in Boston during her husband's absence, he found her in the drawing room, seated at the piano and practicing scales, dressed in a fitted, full skirted, black velvet dress, with an enormous white linen and lace collar and white cuffs, under which she wore a starched white lawn petticoat, trimmed with three rows of lace and the sheerest white cotton panties he'd ever seen. Her opaque white stockings were held up by embroidered garters and on her extremely pretty little feet she wore high heeled black patent leather mary janes. Her blonde hair was pulled back in a black velvet ribbon and she looked demure in it. Michael was touched that she'd gone shopping for the grown up little girl dress just for him. When the time came to fold back her satin lined skirt and white petticoat, he appreciated her attention to detail all the more. And he took great care to spank her only as hard as a little girl should ever be spanked, which was not very hard at all. She melted, of course, though she probably would have benefited from a sound caning even more.

Patricia was much more experimental and adventurous than the other girls he had known, or perhaps she was merely more fearless. Within knowing her two months he had received as presents: a wooden hairbrush, an ivory hairbrush, an English school cane, a razor strop, a Scottish tawse and, unbelievably, a Hermes riding crop. Due to her extremely wise choice of profession, Patricia woke up in luxury hotel suites and lavishly appointed inn cottages at least once a week. So when Michael was handed a beautiful, evocative implement with which to correct the wayward, spoiled young woman, it was often in the most romantic and rarified of settings.

Patricia had no compunction about adopting a room in Michael's house as her own private hideaway, complete with computer, Ralph Lauren daybed and hope chest filled with her own selection of diaphanous night gowns and silk chemises. Patricia was vastly compulsive and she spent a great deal of her time organizing her wardrobe, appointments and men. Michael had no objection to her moving items into his house. It reassured him. All of Damaris' possessions had been picked up and hauled off to the cottage at Pigeon Cove, where she now resided.

It destroyed Patricia's fragile grip on reason to contemplate Michael with Marguerite on one or more of the many nights when she was not with him herself. For Michael had told her, quite firmly, that it was impossible for him to entirely avoid the occasional encounter with Marguerite. Patricia absolutely hated this. She threw horrific tantrums about it. Michael told her that she could obviate the problem by moving in with him, but Patricia did not find that a convenient option. To which Michael had pragmatically replied, "I'm not making any promises I can't keep."

"But, damn it, how many women do you need?" Patricia was working herself up into a passion, pacing across the floor of a private cabin, set up in the wooded hills of an exclusive Nantucket inn.

She strode out to the porch which overlooked a pretty patch of woods, which led down to a pristine white beach. Her fair, slender charms were set off to advantage by a luxuriously embroidered black lace over beige satin peignoir set, fitted close through the torso, with a full skirted gown and magnificently trimmed wrapper. But the Pre-Raphaelite princess spoiled the romantic illusion by sulkily lighting a cigarette.

Sitting with his chin on his hand and an enormous cup of café latte before him, Michael gazed at his terrifyingly willful sweetheart and recalled a phone call he had received while at the station house earlier in the week from The Princess, which was the nickname he had given her in recent weeks to amuse himself when thinking about Patricia. She didn't know about it yet.

They'd exchanged small talk and engaged in the usual flirting when she abruptly interrupted the casual flow of the conversation to interject, "Sometimes I think I'd like to be treated... more harshly."

"Is that so?" Michael's tone did not betray his excitement. Patricia then pretended she had a call on the other line and broke the connection.

All week he had tossed around ideas. He wondered what she meant by the word "harsh." Did she, for instance, want him to handcuff her to a cot in one of the holding cells, thrash her and ravish her? He'd been rather careful until now in the way he played with Patricia. Was it possible that the sort treatment which his ex-wife might have considered too severe, would prove perfectly suitable for Patricia?

"Patricia!" he addressed her in a commanding tone. "Come in here."

Patricia ignored him and continued to smoke, leaning on the railing with her back to Michael. Michael sighed and strode out the balcony. He turned her around, took the cigarette away from her and crushed it out.

"Didn't I call you?"

"So?" she challenged.

Michael took her by the hand and dragged her back inside, picked her oval ebony hairbrush up off a dresser top and sat down on the bed with Patricia across his lap. Without raising her skirts he applied the back of the brush to her bottom a dozen times, hard and fast. Patricia was too conscious of her position as editor of Cape Cod Style to scream at the top of her lungs in a guest cabin at an exclusive Nantucket inn, but she gratified him by immediately bursting into tears. He then pushed her off his lap.

"Why did you do that?" she sobbed, with tears rolling down her face, pulling up her skirts to examine the angry red brush strokes which now decorated her pearly flesh as she knelt on the floor.

"Because you're getting on my nerves."

"I'm sorry," she whimpered. He folded his arms.

"Think your sulks are amusing?"

Patricia dashed away her tears with a petulant shrug.

"You're the most difficult woman I've ever known."

"You must know insipid women," she returned.

"If you're this insolent I must not have spanked you hard enough," Michael observed, picking up the hairbrush again.

"No, please! I'll be good!" she wrapped both arms around one of his legs and rubbed her cheek against it like an ingratiating cat, looking up at him innocently.

Michael couldn't help but laugh. However, after they had gotten dressed and gone out for a walk through the woods to the beach, he spoke his mind to Patricia, telling her that he had no intention of avoiding the occasional encounter with one or more of his few female friends in the scene, including his wife if she ever agreed to see him again. He reminded Patricia that she was married herself and had a whole separate life apart from him, therefore she had little right to restrict his contacts in the town where he lived and she did not. Michael concluded by warning Patricia that he would dissolve their relationship rather than suffer guilt and persecution under her tyranny.

"I see!" Patricia was as hurt and disappointed by Michael's statements as any spoiled child who has been denied a treat. She folded her arms as they walked along, she in a bias cut taupe silk summer dress, he in khaki trousers and a blue chambray shirt.

"How would you feel if I knew all sorts of men in the scene and played with them?" she asked.

"For all I know, you do. Your pain tolerance certainly indicates experience."

Patricia blushed at this observation then scowled, "I keep forgetting that you're a detective."

"But getting back to your question, I wouldn't mind at all if you played with other men. In fact, I think it would help you to feel less insecure about us. I'd be happy to introduce you to some trustworthy players the next time you're in Random Point."

"Fine! So I'm to be passed around among your Castle Roissy buddies, now, am I?"

"Patricia, you know damn well I'm not into a Master trip," he told her, losing patience.

"I don't know any such thing."

"Patricia, you're being willfully obtuse," he declared, stopping in his tracks.

"I am not."

"Suppose I was able to introduce you to a couple of possible playmates for you, without letting them know you're in the scene?"

"I don't understand. To what end?"

"If you liked one you could make the advance yourself at the proper time and place. I wouldn't have to be involved at all."

"But, what would you get out of that?"

"Possibly a more relaxed girlfriend," Michael replied.

"And you wouldn't be jealous?"

"No. And I think it would help our relationship."

"You just want an excuse for your own catting around," she accused.

Michael sighed, "I guess I was dreaming expecting a woman to be rational."

"That's exactly right!" Patricia concurred and no more was said on the subject of new contacts in the scene for the moment.

The next time they met, however, in Random Point the following Friday, Patricia asked Michael to describe the various persons he had in mind to introduce her to. Michael bluntly refused, telling her she was wasting his time, then immediately suggested going antique shopping that afternoon instead. Piqued at having her curiosity denied when she'd been thinking of nothing but Michael's dangerous friends in the scene all week, she assented to the shopping trip in a distracted mood.

Michael was pleased to find Hugo Sands manning his shop when he arrived with Patricia. Hugo was naturally beside himself with joy at the unexpected visit of this important personage in his shop and took some pains to show her his most interesting recent acquisitions.

The editor of Cape Cod Style browsed through the shop with Michael in tow, only subliminally aware that the highly educated proprietor was a good looking man. Thrilled to distraction by Mrs. Fairservis' visit to his establishment, with visions of full color magazine spreads revolving in his practical brain, Hugo barely noticed how beautiful his important guest was, nor did it even remotely occur to him that this media goddess was also an available submissive. Meanwhile, Michael was enjoying his friends' non-reaction to each other and trying to decide who to tell first about the other.

"Hugo, why don't you tempt Mrs. Fairservis with your collection of antique riding crops?" Michael finally said, causing both Hugo and Patricia stop and stare at each other.

"I'd love to, but they're at my house," said Hugo, searching Michael's face for more information. The tall detective simply stared guilelessly back at Hugo. But the remark, after all, had been enough to clue the antique dealer in.

Suddenly realizing that this natty gentleman with the elegant shop and charming manners was one of Michael's friends in the local scene, the blonde girl blushed from brow to throat. She stammered a thank you as Hugo handed her his card, on the back of which he wrote his home phone number.

A few days later Michael got a call at the station while he manned the desk on the late shift.

"Thank you for introducing me to Mrs. Fairservis," Hugo said; "But what's the policy on her?"

"What do you mean?"

"Well, she's made an appointment to come and see the riding crops."

Michael inwardly rejoiced at these words.

"Patricia is my new sweetheart," said Michael.

"Congratulations," said Hugo sincerely, marveling at Michael's good fortune. To get that lucky that fast after losing the divine Damaris was indeed remarkable. Nor did Hugo forget that his adorable ex-assistant, Jane Elliot, with whom he'd had so much fun a few seasons ago, had also come to him through Michael Flagg. He made a note to send Flagg a good bottle of brandy.

"Yes, thank you, and for the most part, it's working out well. She's married, as you know, but so far that hasn't interfered with any of our plans. No, the problem is that for all of her sterling qualities, Patricia is a bit possessive, and I thought that by introducing her to a few local people in the scene it would distract her from fixating on me."

"Good thinking," said Hugo, "and thanks!"

After an appropriate amount of time had elapsed, Michael asked Patricia whether she had seen Hugo yet. They were lying under a large leafy Elm in the long, soft grass of his unweeded back garden which was ringed by the enclosing woods. Patricia was in a full skirted navy halter dress and ankle strap sandals with gold jewelry at her ears, throat and wrists.

"No," she replied, blowing away dandelions.

"Tell me the truth, Patricia," he sat up beside her. Patricia blushed and sat up.

"I said no," she stammered, regretting horribly that she'd begun the lie.

"Patricia, do you want me to turn you over my knee?"

"No!" she sprung to her feet but he captured her wrist before she had a chance to flee and pulled her back down on the grass.

"I think you need a good spanking for lying to me," he told her, pulling her across his lap and bringing his palm down on the seat of her skirt hard and fast several dozen times before pausing to question her again. Patricia, feeling no constraint about noise in their secluded retreat, gave voice to her injured feelings as he spanked her soundly.

"Now, tell me the truth," he ordered.

"Okay, I saw him. I went to his house."

"And did you play?"

"No."

"You're lying," he declared, pulling up her skirt and beginning the spanking all over again, only this time on the seat of her white silk panties. This time he spanked her slower, but harder, until he could see her fair skin color up pink under the sheer briefs.

"All right, we played!" she finally admitted. Michael was pleased to hear this and gently smoothed her skirt back down. He pulled her up and kissed her.

"Don't lie to me again, young lady," he told her sternly. Her lip quivered and she almost cried. He took her down to the grass, pulled her panties off and penetrated her quickly. Face to face, within the first dozen thrusts, Patricia had an orgasm.

For days the thrill of the spontaneous spanking he had given her, and the firmness of the sex which had followed, caused spasms of pleasure to ripple through her flat little tummy. Patricia adored Michael. He was everything she had always looked for in a man. He looked the right way and said the right things. And he punished her so beautifully. So correctly. Patricia was in love.

Patricia was so extraordinarily compulsive that Michael dared hope she was anal, though at first she would only admit to entertaining vague fantasies. She seemed afraid of anal sex with him because of the size of his cock. However, the first time he inserted a finger into her bottom while she lay across his lap, Patricia ground against his trousered thigh until she came, and this didn't take long.

Encouraged, he became more inventive.

One Friday night, when Michael found it impossible to drive into Boston to be with her, he'd had a terrible argument with Patricia over the phone. She'd thrown one of her usual tantrums and he'd responded by hanging up. For an hour or two he was fed up with Patricia and vowed not to call her again for a week. However, when she phoned him at the station house at midnight to tearfully apologize, he felt touched by her childish needs.

"If I drive into the city tomorrow," he told her sternly, "it will only be to punish you."

"I understand," she sighed, ashamed of her own immaturity, yet perversely excited by the concept of really being punished.

When Michael arrived at Patricia's house in Back Bay the following evening he curtly told her to put on a short black dress and heels. When she took too long a time in selecting her outfit, Michael turned her under his arm and smacked her hard about a dozen times. The sharp blows brought tears to her eyes. Michael wasn't smiling when he let her go.

Patricia hastily chose a black jersey sheath, black seamed stockings, garter belt and black patent leather ankle strap stiletto heels. While she was dressing in her large, walk in closet, Michael sat on the bed and placed his handkerchief, containing a certain object, beside him.

"Patricia," Michael said, "Don't come back in here without the KY."

Patricia shivered in fear and excitement on the other side of the door. Presently she obeyed his command, standing before him in her clinging dress, all silky blonde hair and slim legs. Michael unceremoniously pulled her down across his knees and pushed her tight dress up to her hips. Her sheer, full black briefs encased her luminous white bottom with the flawless radiance of a Varga gatefold. He eased these down at once and left them bunched around her knees. Now her garter belt framed her bare bottom so prettily that he couldn't help but spank her.

"I'm disappointed in you, Patricia," he told her. "You should know better than to distract me with nonsense while I'm on duty."

"I'm sorry!" she vowed sincerely, since he'd begun to smack her bottom vigorously.

"You're a very bad, very spoiled little girl," he declared, separating her thighs as far as the bunched briefs would allow. "Hold your legs apart, Patricia."

Patricia gave a tiny sob and complied to the best of her ability, feeling terribly ashamed. He reached for the lube and she placed it in his hand. Tossing the cap aside, Michael plunged the open tube between her satiny bottom cheeks and squeezed out a quantity of clear jelly. This done, he unwrapped from handkerchief a brand new 5" retention plug, cast in flesh colored rubber.

"See this, Patricia?" he brandished it in front of her. She gasped in shame. "I'm going to insert this in your bottom and then we're going out."

"No! You can't! Please don't!" she begged and twisted on his lap. Relentlessly, Michael separated her cheeks and placed the tip of the plug in between them.

"You've been asking for some real discipline for awhile. Haven't you, young lady?" he spread her open with one hand while inserting the butt plug into her, quite agonizingly slowly.

"God, no! You can't do this to me!" she protested weakly, trying to fend him off with one hand. This he grabbed and smacked as though she were a naughty child.

"Lie still. You don't need a boyfriend, you need a master."

"Oh, please, darling, stop! I can't stand it, I tell you. If you continue doing this, I'm going to come!"

"Whether you do or don't, I intend to take you out." he told her.

But Patricia didn't come. The whole experience was so humiliating that she could think of nothing but escaping it. She begged and cajoled Michael to remove the toy and let her go. Instead, he pushed it in deeper, until all but the hilt was buried in her bottom. Then he pulled her panties off.

"You know what? Just to enhance the sensation, don't you have a shiny black long line panty girdle?" Michael had a very good memory for hiding places and strode immediately to the proper dresser and even the right drawer. He soon discovered the ultra tight, retro knickers which were trimmed with black lace at each leg hole. Once on they came to just above her knees and hugged her slender thighs and oval cheeks like latex. "They're almost a form of bondage," he declared, turning her around between his hands, and examining her lithe bottom and legs from every angle as she blushed with shame.

Simply to amuse himself he bent her over his knee again and spanked her lightly over the long line panty girdle which had become so popular with the Victoria's Secret crowd lately. She felt desperately humiliated whenever he patted the center of her bottom, exactly atop the deeply anchored retention plug.

Michael held her by her slim waist as he tormented her with a mild but embarrassing spanking.

"This is a very smart garment," he commented, "and perfect for holding your retention plug firmly in place." He punctuated this declaration with a volley of one dozen sharp smacks across the center of her upturned bottom, seeming to drive the plug in deeper with each fresh blow. As he spanked her he worked his free hand around and under her tummy to cup her throbbing pussy in the palm of his hand while spanking her with the other.

"No, please!" Patricia cried.

"Don't fight it, Patricia," he told her. "You're finally getting the attention you crave." Michael held her fast and spanked her harder. But then he quite abruptly let her up.

"I've decided to postpone your orgasm," he told her, because he wanted to keep her in the perfect dildo bondage. "Put yourself together now, we're going." Michael said.

Patricia looked momentarily mutinous, but Michael stared her down with a look that jellified her spine. Finally she turned to comply with his command, but he pulled her back around to face him.

"Were you about to rebel, Patricia?"

She lowered her eyes sullenly. Michael took her by the wrist and slapped the back of her hand, then forced her to look at him and slapped it again, harder. Tears sprang immediately to her eyes as she pressed her prettily manicured little hand to her flushed face like a four year old who has just been summarily disciplined and is about to burst into tears.

"Don't defy me," he told her sternly. Her lower lip quivered, then she tried to hide her face behind her hands. He pulled them away from her face. Seeing that she was about to cry he pulled her against him and held her. "It's all right, Patricia," he soothed her, fearing that he was breaking her down too fast.

Michael kissed her and continued doing so until the danger of her bursting into tears had passed. Then he repeated the command to get her jacket.

"I can't possibly go out like this!" she protested.

"Why not?" he stared back at her.

"I'll die of shame."

"No you won't."

"Please don't make me go out like this," she begged. Ignoring her, he himself got her short leather jacket and put her into it as he would a recalcitrant child.

"We are going out, just like this, and what's more, we're going to do some really sleazy things, starting with a trip to The Pleasure Chest to buy you a proper harness."

"No!"

"I love the way you haven't stopped blushing," he said, escorting her out into the balmy May night.

Patricia bit her lip in vexation as he refused the keys to her Mercedes and instead hailed a cab on the street.

"Public transportation will be good enough for Princess tonight," Michael informed her.

Patricia endured the reckless taxi drive downtown in humiliated silence, with eyes turned toward the window. When ever she looked at him, however, each fresh glimpse of his sternly masculine demeanor would cause her tummy to contract.

Michael insinuated his hand under her dress to caress and separate her thighs in the tight panty girdle. He pressed his palm against her lower abdomen and pubic mound through the stretch lycra.

"Don't think you won't get another spanking once I get you home, young lady," Michael said, without paying the slightest attention to the cab driver, who appeared to have barely enough English to understand directions. However, Patricia noticed his liquid, Middle Eastern eyes perk up with interest in the mirror at the key word "spanking."

At the Pleasure Chest Michael did not consult Patricia about any of their purchases. The graceful lady's torso harness was made of black leather, and trimmed with stainless steel studs. It was adjustable and slit at the crotch and seat in order to accommodate one or two dildos and hold them in place. The belt could be pulled tight enough to snugly fit a slender woman. Patricia stood by with burning cheeks as Michael discussed in great detail the subtleties of the device with the helpful gay male clerk. Together they chose the perfect pair of vibrators to slip into the slots of the harness and then moved on to additional accessories. Michael summarily rejected nipple clamps, ball gags, and dilators but accepted a large, cased set of textured dildos intended for anal stimulation. He also purchased two pair of leather cuffs, suitable for binding wrists and ankles, boat hooks for fastening them, as well as two stainless steel spreader bars, designed to fully or partially spread-eagle a playmate. Next a variety of exotic lubricants were selected. A black leather blindfold and a multi-thonged flogger, which was a kind of whip with broad, supple lashes, also joined the pile of costly fittings on the counter top.

The only item which Patricia protested was a cheap French maid's outfit which Michael fingered momentarily on their way out of the shop. "No way in hell," she murmured at the cut and texture. Michael smiled at the fussy little perfectionist who would accept two dildos and a harness with very little protest but who would have thrown a ballistic tantrum had he actually tried to force her into a tacky polyester maid's outfit.

Hailing another cab, Michael then took Patricia into the seedy Combat Zone, where strip clubs and adult books stores and hooker hotels abounded.

"Michael, I don't like it around here," she said. He had left the bag of toys in the cab and told the driver to wait, showing him his badge to make sure that he did.

"Don't worry about it," he told her, with the confidence of a cop in the city he grew up in.

The disinterested clerk behind the high counter at the adult video and magazine store barely looked up as they entered. Michael picked out a hard S&M video from B & D Pleasures to rent and they retired together to a private viewing booth at the back of the store.

Once they got into the booth Michael sat in the chair, unzipped his trousers and released his large, throbbing erection, quite casually.

"Take the knickers off now," he commanded. Eyes locked with his, she obeyed. Not wanting to put them down anywhere, she held them in one hand as he pulled her down to sit on his lap, facing away from him and towards the screen. "Lean forward," he told her, holding her around her slender waist with one and hand attempting to guide his cock into her pussy with the other. "One way or another, this is happening, so you'd better concentrate on getting it in at the right angle," he softly suggested.

Patricia was outraged and deeply aroused. She'd never had a masterful lover but her mind had thrilled to the thought of one since her very early teens. Now she was getting the attention she had craved, just as Michael had said. So naturally Patricia was wet enough to slide it in. And as it did go in, all the way in, as Patricia leaned forward against his encircling arm. The retention plug, meanwhile, was still firmly lodged in her bottom, so that when Michael's cock completely filled her, she experienced double penetration. Once she was settled snugly down on his lap, he brought his left hand around to press on her lower abdomen and pull her back against him hard each time she drifted slightly forward. His other arm, meanwhile, was still locked around her waist, to anchor her to his lap while her beautiful legs straddled his.

"Now this is what we're going to do, Patricia," he whispered in her ear. "You're going to lean back now and grind against me and your plug like the naughty girl that you are while I keep the palm of my hand flat against your clit until you come. Understand?"

"Yes, sir," she dared to breathe.

"Then, I'm going to," he told her.

It happened just as he predicted, with a sharp little smack against her outer thigh sending her over the edge. Then, almost as soon as her spasms began to subside, Michael fastened both hands to her waist and effortlessly bounced her light body up and down on an engine that was now in danger of overheating until a large, boiling emission threatened to burst inside her clinging sheath. At the very last moment he lifted Patricia off his lap and pulling his penis free, ejaculated harmlessly against her satiny bottom cheeks as he pulled her back against him. Neither of them had bothered to glance at the screen for more than a moment or two but once they were done both of them felt as though they'd been to a hell of a movie together.

After the incident at the Combat Zone book store, where Michael and Patricia had rented but not watched a bondage and discipline video, Patricia became deeply infatuated with her long distance lover. The youthful detective exactly conformed to her ideal of masculine charm. Michael was not overbearing. He had no apparent interest in interfering with any portion of her life. Even his sexual dominance over her was restrained in Patricia's perception, though Flagg at first worried that he sometimes went too far.

Patricia had a large tolerance for corporal punishment. She was also a terrible brat. She knew she needed a thrashing every couple of days and went out of her way to make sure one came to her.

Patricia presented Michael with his first cane, his first tawse and his first heavy wooden paddle. And he did truly enjoy inflicting hard corporal punishment on a young lady who so desperately craved it.

But even more interesting to him was the combined effect of sound spanking and embarrassment, upon a woman of Patricia's temperament.

He had taken home the purchases from the Boston sex shop, including the harness and laid these items aside for a future significant encounter.

Ever since Michael had introduced Hugo to Patricia she had become 90% more circumspect about reproaching him for his interest in other women. Congratulating himself that he was finally able to outsmart a woman, he now enjoyed almost complete peace of mind with regard to their relationship. However, an annoying 10% of the time, Patricia continued to persecute him relentlessly about all of the Random Point girls. Except Laura.

Patricia had only run into Laura once, by accident, when Laura had decided to visit Michael's house to flirt. Naturally Patricia's alarms went off when she took in all of Laura Random's quiet charms and effectively frightened the native away with a steely glance. Laura had no wish to get into a cat fight with a jealous, high strung woman over a man who would probably live in her neighborhood all of her life. So Laura wasn't seen again in that part of the woods behind Random Point until Michael called her himself, with Patricia at his side, several weeks later, with an unusual request, especially coming from him.

Patricia was visiting for the evening and realized too late that she had left her pot in Boston. Boldly and without the slightest hesitation or shame, Patricia began to pester Michael about finding her some grass in the village. Michael immediately thought of two girls, his ex-wife and Laura.

"I could call Laura," he said casually. Normally he did not approve of drug use and shuddered at the thought of abetting it, but weighing the positive benefits of presenting Patricia with a trustworthy girlfriend in the scene, he overcame his scruples and made the suggestion.

"Would she bring some over, do you think?" Patricia seemed to forget that she was ever jealous of Laura.

"It's a possibility, but let me think about it for a minute. Do I really want to encourage this sort of behavior... ?" he mused.

In the end, he called Laura and she arrived with supplies for Patricia within the half hour. The two girls went out into the woods together to smoke and since it was a warm May evening, lingered there until the sun went down. When they returned Michael threatened to spank them both for being so naughty, but Laura merely smiled and went home.

Patricia now had a girlfriend in the village, to bring her information and to confide in. Laura was so frank with Patricia about her admiration for Michael that Patricia no longer feared her. Laura understood and respected the fact that Patricia was now Michael's girlfriend. As it happened, Laura was just as happy to have a new girlfriend, with whom she had so much in common.

For some time now Laura had been experiencing a pleasant urge to play games with another woman. Girls like Marguerite and Damaris were somehow too close, almost like sisters she knew them so well, but Patricia seemed just right. Her education was on a par with Laura's and Patricia had style. She also seemed very submissive and the budding imp of dominance in Laura's personality responded to that.

From the start they behaved more like playmates than regular girlfriends. Patricia would never return to Random Point without a beautiful present for Laura. And Laura would never visit Patricia without a tasty treat tucked into her pocket. One day Laura smacked Patricia on the bottom.

They were in the big, well furnished kitchen on the ground floor of Anthony Newton's Cape Cod house, where Laura had resided since leaving her husband. They had been fixing a snack and Patricia looked so cute leaning over the sink in her Guess jeans that Laura couldn't resist.

Patricia looked at her with a rush of passion that almost frightened Laura and said, "If you're going to do it, girlfriend, do it right."

"All right," said Laura, pulling out a kitchen chair of the perfect height and stability and pulling Patricia down across her own denim thighs.

Grasping Patricia firmly about the waist Laura felt a curious thrill. So this was what it felt like to be William or Michael or Hugo or Anthony. All the men she knew and were fond of had experienced this sensation with her. They had looked down to see a slender, sweetly compliant girl stretched across their lap, with her bottom upturned for a spanking. It felt extremely satisfying to bring her hand down smartly on Patricia's slim, muscular bottom, so snugly encased in the jeans. The smacks made a luscious sound to Laura's ears and a surge of vicarious pleasure shot through the core of her sex as she remembered what she liked about being in this position and tried to provide exactly that for Patricia.

"I'm doing this," Laura advised her captive, who looked back at Laura over one bare shoulder in her red gingham halter top.

"Why do you want to?"

"I just want to." Laura explained, smoothing the seat of Patricia's jeans with her palm before bringing it down on her bottom again and continuing with the spanking.

Patricia enjoyed the spanking over her jeans for the next fifteen minutes without saying another word. When it was over and Laura let her up, Patricia could barely prevent herself from handing Laura an implement, craving more and harder spanking now from her pretty, dark haired friend. But Patricia was too embarrassed to ask for more and in fact, blushed for at least an hour following her first spanking from another girl. Also, her bottom felt warm and tingly under her jeans for what seemed like an hour after the spanking, though it hadn't seemed at all that hard at the time. Laura realized, towards the end of the spanking, that she had to bring her hand all the way up before bringing it down, in order to make a good impression on a girl who was used to being disciplined by a 6'3" man. This was invigorating.

Later, Laura told Patricia that Patricia was the first girl she had ever taken across her lap, though she admitted to having nuzzled the ears and throat of Damaris Flagg and clasped her about the waist several times when they were working together in her husband's office the previous summer. Patricia suffered whenever she heard about Damaris because she never heard anything but good of her and she knew that Michael still loved her dearly.

Patricia and Laura began to play regularly but made a compact not to let the boys know about it. To Hugo and Michael, they were simply compatible girl friends. But when Patricia and Laura were alone, Laura always wore trousers and always sought to dominant her pretty blonde friend. Laura was enthralled by Patricia's accessibility and responsiveness. Every time they played they went a little further. First the skirt came up. Then next time the panties came down. And the time after that, Laura's sensitive fingers sought the source of Patricia's excitement. And the time after that, Laura forced Patricia to climax. It was all innocent fun but somehow the girls felt more secure in keeping it to themselves.

Once Patricia had acquired Laura as a friend and playmate, her insecurities were further reduced. She had very little time to be jealous between all of these interesting new friends. When the girls were together they spent most of their time discussing the men they played with and the things they did with them.

Patricia admired Michael's cool headedness in arranging her sex life for her so as to cancel out any playing he might do. In each of her past relationships, including her present marriage, she had always been able to easily manipulate her men. This time it was different. In many ways, Michael was more sophisticated than she and he expected her to rise to his level of understanding.

As the spring progressed, Michael began to notice an improvement in Patricia's attitude. She scarcely seemed jealous anymore. But this was mainly because she knew that Michael never saw his ex-wife.

Michael began to explore some of his more esoteric fantasies with Patricia. One afternoon, they were enjoying a full tea at a charming Vermont inn, when Patricia insisted that she had to go out into the garden and have a cigarette. Michael barely seemed to notice, as he was working the Sunday crossword, but when Patricia returned he mildly admonished her, saying, "With your toxic lifestyle, dearest, you really ought to be cleansing regularly."

Their blue eyes locked as she regained her seat, his serious gaze causing her tummy to contract. "What do you mean?" she appeared confused, but her blush indicated full comprehension of his statement.

"I'll be happy to show you. And you'll feel much better for it," Michael promised.

"Really, I could never endure it," she protested, her face flaming now.

"Why not?" he reached for her hand and enclosed it in his. "Do you think I would suggest this if I didn't know what I was doing?"

"But, what would you get out of it?"

"You always ask me that," he smiled.

"I've fantasized about it," she admitted, but I really couldn't bear the embarrassment."

"You'd enjoy the hell out of it."

"No!"

"Never mind. I'll take care of you just fine. We'll do it in our attic room. And I checked - there's no one below us tonight. So I can probably give you a sound spanking as well."

Then Michael gaily went off to the village to purchase what he needed. Patricia spent the afternoon in an ecstasy of painful anticipation. Right before dinner they walked in the woods and Michael administered a hard spanking over her beige chiffon summer dress which clung to every elegant curve of her torso and thighs like fairy wrapping. He had found a stump to sit down on and Patricia fit across his thighs perfectly.

"I can't spank you very long or hard at the inn, Patricia, so I think I'll do both now."

Patricia always loved being over Michael's knee in the woods. A long, hard spanking over her dress, slip and panties left a subtle sting that lingered for hours.

All through the splendid gourmet dinner, which they ate in a beautiful wood beamed room overlooking a waterfall, Patricia remembered the few minutes in the woods, along with the feel of his big hand coming down on the back of her skirt. Across the table he looked handsome and mild. But when he caught her looking at him in that dreamy and distracted way she had, he frowned sternly.

"Don't drink too much wine," he warned. "You're being punished tonight."

Patricia stared at him wide-eyed.

"You do remember what we discussed earlier, don't you, Patricia?"

"No!" she lowered her eyes willfully and tossed her glass of wine down.

"You're a self indulgent child," he told her. "You need discipline." He squeezed her thigh under the table, then reached between her thighs to lightly probe her through her panties. Her panties were already wet from the spanking over his knee in the woods. Patricia pushed his hand away with a furious blush. Michael smiled and ceased to torment her for the remainder of their meal.

After playing one game of backgammon in the parlor, Michael told Patricia it was time to go upstairs. He marched her up in front of him. When they reached the isolated attic honeymoon suite he locked the door behind them. A skylight admitted moonlight and a glimpse of stars. Two low lamps had also been lit but otherwise the ambiance was sleepy and intimate.

The large, adjoining bath was particularly sexy, of Italian design, with black marble and cherry wood furnishings and a free standing claw footed antique copper tub, with vintage taps and modern hose and shower attachments. Beside the tub stood a tall, well stocked wooden towel stand.

When Michael took Patricia upstairs he ordered to her take a long, hot bath and then put on her sheer, white Egyptian cotton night gown and robe set, which was fitted through the torso but full through the skirt.

While Patricia was cautiously bathing, Michael entered, rolled up his sleeves and wordlessly began to bathe her, squeezing the hot sponge over her breasts and back and gently soaping her there for a long time, unless the tension began to visibly recede from her shoulders.

After her bath she slipped into the shower stall to rinse off. When she came out Michael helped to dry her and put her into her nightgown and robe. The tint of her skin was revealed through the gauzy material.

Michael firmly bent Patricia over the marble sink and pulled her skirts up to her waist.

"Spread you legs apart," he told her, reaching into a cabinet for a leather bag he had placed there earlier in the day. "Arch you back and present your bottom to me," he added, ready to instantly punish the slightest hesitation. Michael had positioned them opposite a full length mirror, set in the fancy wooden towel closet door. "Patricia, if you turn your head just a bit to the left you can see what I'm doing to you," he suggested while inserting his right hand into a sterile latex glove.

Patricia stole one glance then turned her head away.

"Don't you want to see?"

"No!"

"Pay attention, Patricia, or I'll spank you," he advised. So she forced herself to watch as he produced a tube of lubricant and began to penetrate her bottom with the middle finger of his gloved hand. "Arch your bottom higher and don't contract," he ordered, using his free hand to divide her satiny white cheeks. He screwed his finger in and out several times before withdrawing it completely and discarding the glove. "Stand up," he told her. Patricia turned to face him, blushing deeply. Michael pulled her to him and kissed her. Then he made her look at him. "Are you embarrassed, Patricia?"

She bit her lip and turned away.

"You need to be disciplined," he reiterated. "Now fill the bathtub again with very warm water and plenty of bubbles."

After Patricia started the soft water running from the graceful antique spigots, Michael took her across his lap as he sat on a varnished wooden bench.

"What are you doing?" she trembled.

"While we're waiting for the tub to fill up I'm going to examine you and take your temperature," he informed her, separating her thighs as much as possible and gently probing her now creamy sex. "You're very wet," he told her unnecessarily. "The treatment is already conferring benefits on you."

Withdrawing two dripping fingers from her pussy, he dried them on a fluffy white towel and produced a thermometer. Still extremely well lubricated, Patricia felt no discomfort as he inserted it into her anus and then held it in place as the bath tub continued to fill.

"It's a shame that none of your many lovers ever cared enough about you to do something like this, but I'll make up for that neglect," Michael promised, patting her bare bottom kindly. Patricia groaned in a torment of excitement, fervently agreeing with his observation.

"Thank you," she murmured, a meek little blue eyed lamb for once.

"My dear, you have a shockingly high temperature," he informed her presently. "I can see we're just in time here."

Once the tub was filled with creamy bubbles Michael had Patricia strip completely naked and climb back in. He then positioned her with her elbows leaning comfortably on the rim of the tub while kneeling with her upturned bottom thrusting up through the foam. Michael knelt in front of her momentarily to show her the hot water bag.

"See this, Patricia? I'm going to fill this with warm water. It holds about two quarts. And give you an enema. This is the nozzle," he indicated the long, multi-perforated white plastic nozzle which attached to a hose and then connected to the black rubber bag. "You're very well lubricated. Do you think this will be any problem for you?"

"No, sir," she replied, blushing again and averting her eyes while throbbing with excitement.

"You're being such a good girl about this," he complimented her, kissing her lightly on the lips before filling the bag and suspending it well above the tub on the handy wooden tallboy which had been provided for hanging bath blankets on.

When he was quite ready to insert the nozzle into her bottom, Michael told her to spread her thighs as much as possible and open her bottom to him. Patricia became painfully aroused as it penetrated her inch by inch until the entire 5" nozzle had disappeared into her rectum and only the hose protruded from her bottom, which tightly contracted around it.

Michael released the clamp and warm water began to flow into her bottom, causing an intensely pleasurable yet profoundly humiliating reaction to ripple through her.

"We'll start with just a little at a time," he said, closing off the flow and taking a few moments to check and adjust the position of the hose as it protruded from her bare, soapy bottom and reach under the water to briefly cup her public mound in his hand, then pass his palm under her tummy to explore its gentle swell. Patricia moaned, half dizzy with pleasure.

Before beginning the flow again Michael administered a half dozen smacks to her vulnerable bottom. They were baby smacks, barely hard enough to sting, but in combination with the anal intrusion, the spanking made Patricia whimper.

"You see, darling? Obedient girls receive very mild spankings."

He released the clamp again and the water once again began to fill her tummy. “Now, Patricia, I want you to notice the mirror above the bathtub. That’s right, just raise your head and you’ll see it.”

Patricia couldn’t avoid acknowledging the oval mirror suspended over the bath in such a way as to reveal her soapy, glistening bottom, now forced to accommodate the rubber hose. How many mirrors could one bathroom need? She couldn’t look for long. It was much too intense to feel and to see at the very same time.

“Do you know why you have to be treated like this, Patricia?” Michael finished administering the enema.

“No,” she whimpered.

“Because you need to learn some self control. Now hold completely still while I remove the nozzle,” he recommended, then adroitly withdrew the long plastic tube from her bottom. Patricia groaned.

Michael helped her out of the tub and dried her completely before wrapping her in the white gown and robe. Then he took her across his knee and bared her bottom. Producing a standard 5” rubber retention plug, he divided her cheeks and attempted to insert the well lubricated tip, into her tightly contracted anus.

“Relax and let me do this,” he told her.

“I’m afraid to!”

“Nonsense. I told you that you’re going to learn some self control. You’re going to retain your first enema for at least 15 minutes and naturally you will have a retention plug inserted into your bottom for the entire time.”

“I understand,” she replied, trembling at the sternness in his voice.

Michael re-lubricated the rubber plug, separated her cheeks with his fingers and plunged the flexible dildo in between them. This time it slipped immediately up into her bottom. He held it in place with his hand for a minute while she lay across his lap, passive now as an obedient child.

Presently he began to spank her on her bare, firmly plugged bottom. Patricia felt shameful pleasure and wriggled on his lap.

“Of course you need to receive at least two enemas for the treatment to be even slightly effective,” he informed her, while smacking her bottom just a bit harder. “So you’re getting a second one shortly. And you’ll be expected to hold that one longer, I’m afraid.” The smacks fell rhythmically, on one cheek then the other, then across the middle, right atop the plug, driving it in if it ever slipped out. Once it all but popped out and Michael pretended to be angry at her lack of control. “You’re not paying attention, Patricia!” he scolded, pulling it all the way out, then carefully plunging it back in to the hilt. Once more he repeated this. “Don’t you dare let it slip out again,” he warned, again withdrawing the retention plug completely before completely reinserting it into her tight, slippery bottom. These humiliating attentions rapidly achieved the desired effect of causing Patricia to have a long, intensely satisfying climax across his lap.

Patricia was then allowed one hour to herself before Michael promised to return and administer the second course of the treatment. He went for a walk around the grounds and found it difficult to cool off even in the brisk evening air. She was a marvelous girl.

Given such a luxurious amount of time Patricia was able to see to her most urgent bodily demands, shower and regain 90% of her dignity in a fresh peignoir set and then was even able to get high. Michael was not happy about this when he returned.

“Patricia, haven’t you learned anything? You’re supposed to be undergoing a detox treatment this evening. Smoking in the middle is counterproductive.”

“Damn it!” Patricia pretended to curse her own weakness.

“And I really don’t know why you bothered to put a whole new outfit on,” he continued to complain, summarily depriving her of a pristine blue cotton wrapper. “The other one was barely damp from your excitement. I really don’t know what I’m going to do with you,” he turned her under his arm and spanked her bottom soundly through the light nightgown. “You have to conquer this compulsion you have to constantly change your clothes,” he told her. He finished up with six hard smacks. “Don’t make me tell you that again,” he said, setting her back on her feet, in the fresh, exquisitely fitted night gown.

“You haven’t learned anything at all about self control yet,” he lamented, producing the leather harness he had bought her in Boston, along with two vibrators. “Don’t be alarmed, Patricia. This is for your own good."

"What are you going to do now?"

"Now I'm going to put you into your harness and administer your second enema. Only this one will be a Bardex. Leave the gown here and meet me back in the bathroom."

While Patricia fastened the straps of the leather body harness around her naked torso, Michael prepared her second enema with a fuller bag. When he was ready for her, he positioned the broad wooden bench and towel valet adjacent to each other and suspended the hot water bag from the top peg, as before. Laying out what he needed beside him on the bench, he took Patricia across his lap and positioned her comfortably.

"Arch up," he told her, lubricating one of the vibrators and gently inserting it into the leather slit atop her vagina. The dildo slid up into her creamy pussy with embarrassing ease. Patricia's face burned with shame at Michael's small laugh at this. He patted it into place and anchored it there by means of a leather strap attached to the harness and looped to the vibrator through a special hook. "The harness should hold that in place nicely throughout the coming ordeal," Michael promised. "I won't turn it on just yet."

Next he showed her the Bardex nozzle.

"This is to help you retain your enema without a plug," he explained, causing her to blush and sob. "Yes, I know it's embarrassing even to discuss such things, but please remember that if you were a good girl I would never have to resort to such measures. I told you that you had to learn some discipline. The nozzle goes in deeply, then the bulb inflates inside your bottom, to seal the water in without you even thinking about it. Understand?"

Patricia nodded. Michael lubricated her anus and spread it with his fingers. Then he inserted the nozzle slowly into her rectum. It took a long time to go in all the way and Patricia wriggled involuntarily as the penetration continued. Once it was in completely in, he inflated the bulb inside her. She had to make her mind a blank in order not to come again.

He began to give her the enema a little at a time. It felt very warm as it filled her. She took the entire bag without a protest. Michael patted her bottom softly as the last few drops filtered in.

"Now, young lady, I expect you to behave yourself for a least twenty minutes this time. And I believe I promised you a sound spanking as well."

Keeping her firmly anchored across his lap, with the enema hose still protruding from her delicious white buttocks, he began to paddle Patricia with a small, wooden pocket paddle he produced.

Patricia writhed with pleasure and shame across her lover's thighs, her small tummy filled with hot water and her bottom tightly plugged.

"Dearest, things are about to become a bit more extreme now," Michael warned her, before giving the top of the vibrator a twist and starting it vibrating in her pussy. He pressed down on her bottom gently as he also adjusted the hose still depending from her bottom. "You know, Patricia," he advised her, "After you're thoroughly cleaned out and fully recovered from the multiple orgasms you're about to have, sometime around dawn, when you're just waking up, I intend to slip my cock into your bottom and take you properly there."

Michael listened closely to the small inarticulate noises issuing from Patricia's parted lips and shut the vibrator off.

"Hold still," he told her, deflating the bulb and very slowly withdrawing the Bardex nozzle from her bottom. Laying this apparatus aside he showed her the other vibrator, a 7" model, slightly thinner around than the one he had inserted into her vagina. Lubricating the plastic dildo as well as her anus, which was accessible only through the slit in the harness, he inserted it into her bottom, slowly and as deeply as it could go. Finally only one inch of hilt protruded from the harness slit which targeted her anus so cunningly and Patricia was as completely filled as she had ever been.

Much too humiliated to utter a sound, Patricia abandoned herself to the sensation of having her pussy and bottom stuffed with large dildos while her tummy was filled with warm water and her dominant lover held her firmly across his lap. She sobbed and bit her knuckle. It was really too much! If he did just one more thing she would climax immediately.

Michael held her by the waist and began to spank her soundly. "This is just what you need, young lady," he told her, bringing his palm down hard on her fully exposed buttocks until her fair complexion was tinged a dark pink. Then he paused and activated the vibrator he had inserted into her bottom. Michael held her firmly in place and resumed spanking her vigorously until she came, which happened almost immediately.

After her spasms died away, which took quite some minutes, Michael lay her down on the bench, extracted the dildo from her vagina and replaced it with his own cock. Still plugged from behind, Patricia accepted this new mode of intercourse with shy curiosity.

"But what if it slips out!" she worried as he drove in to the hilt and started to deliberately pump her.

"If it slips out you'll be severely punished," he warned, in a tone which caused her to have a third climax. Gratified at this unusual degree of responsiveness, he did not prolong his own release, which of course had been pending for the last two hours.

Later that night, as they lay in the moonlight, Michael cradled Patricia in his arms. She was very sleepy.

"You see, you do feel better now, don't you, Patricia?"

"Much better, thank you."

Chapter Five

Winter on the Hudson

After her infatuation with Michael Flagg had exhausted itself, Susan promised herself that she would try to be good for the rest of the year. Then the incident occurred in the library. Susan was seated at a table in a long gallery, with her books spread out around her, when she noticed, out of the corner of her eye, some papers spread out on the next table, including an envelope with a familiar letterhead.

Susan made sure that no one was around before walking up to the table and taking a really close look at the envelope, which was identical to the one in which her favorite spanking magazine came delivered. Whoever was sitting at that table was a subscriber, just as she was, to Hugo Sands' quarterly journal. Susan wondered whether she should say something as soon as the girl came back. Surely the young lady would be thrilled to discover a kindred spirit here. Susan sat down to take notes on English history.

About twenty minutes later a tall sandy haired boy she knew well from the drama department came and sat down at the table, not noticing her across the way.

Marcus Gower was handsome, with smoky blue eyes, a wide mouth and a lean physique. He came from a wealthy New York family and was the darling of the drama department. Marcus was popular with all women and girls. He was active on the newspaper, the debating club and the men's track team. He was lazy lidded and cynical, but was also warm, clever, quick to tease and on good terms with everyone. When he cleaned up smartly and put on a suit, except for the length of his hair, he could have passed for an usher at a Republican fund raiser. Dressed down, he looked like a rock star.

Marcus had strong ambitions to go on the stage and managed to garner a plum role in every campus production.

Susan stared at him in fascination. Of course she had seen him around, but had never entertained a fantasy about him, except for two hours one afternoon when she was painting flats on set crew for a play in which he had a role, and had overheard him scolding an actress in the cast for not making it to rehearsal the previous night. The tone in which he used the word "young lady" had made Susan's tummy clench with that certain feeling.

Feeling her eyes on him, Marcus looked up and gave Susan his standard, off the shelf, charm a pretty girl smile, vaguely recognizing her from set crew, then began to read again. Susan felt her face grow warm as she wrote a letter to Anthony on her pink legal pad.

"Dear Anthony," it read, *"There has been an interesting development around here which I thought I would consult you about before pursuing.*

It appears there is a boy in my class whom I find attractive and who is without a doubt into it. I will never be able to resist testing him now that I've been made aware of his proclivities. I know you will understand this and hope you will give me permission to be just a little bit naughty while you are away next month in sunny California signing movie contracts.

Love,
Susan"

Anthony called her as soon as he got the letter and left a message on her answering machine, telling her to, "Go for it." In the two days which passed while she was waiting for this reply, Susan planned her strategy. She had been tracking the movements of Marcus around the campus, as girls will do when they get a crush on a boy, when she began to realize that a bold confrontation would not put her at any particular advantage. He was too popular, too used to pretty girls encouraging conversations with him to be dazzled by one more petite, blue eyed blonde. So she decided to return to her time honored method of writing a letter.

Perching in a tower window seat of the Gothic library, while snow began to fall outside in the dark, when she ought to have been reading Don Quixote, Susan wrote:

Dear Marcus,

You don't know me. I'm just a girl in one of your classes. But I think we may have an important interest in common. I only know this because I happened to see you with an envelope bearing the distinctive return address of a company in Random Point, MA, from which I also get mailings and buy magazines.

Ordinarily I would never approach a stranger as I'm doing now, but there are so few of us around that perhaps you will forgive my forwardness on this occasion. I know that you are very popular and socialize with many girls, but are any of them into it?

If any of this is interesting to you, call me at ___

Susan

She put it in the campus mail that evening. He would get it first thing in the morning.

At exactly eleven thirty the following morning, about an hour after the mail was up, Susan's phone rang in her room. Her heart jumped as she picked it up.

"Susan?" Marcus had a fine, distinctive voice, it was also one which women found sexy.

"Yes, who's this?"

"The person you sent the letter to."

"Oh!"

"You remember the letter?"

"Oh yes."

"It gave me quite a start."

"Did you find it interesting?"

"It's the most interesting letter I've ever gotten. When can I meet you?"

"You want to meet me?"

"Who are you? Which class are you in?"

"Maybe I'll keep you guessing for a while."

"Come on, now, Susan, don't be coy. You wrote to me, after all."

"That's true," she hesitated. "But perhaps you won't like me."

"I already like you."

"Perhaps you won't be attracted to me," she said.

"I'm already attracted to you."

"Perhaps my looks won't appeal to you," she said, looking at herself in the mirror opposite her bed, where she lay on her back in her size 5 blue jeans and a fitted cream wool shirt, her thick blonde hair in her usual high pony tail with one lug soled leather ankle boot balanced atop a knee.

"Why? What do you look like?" he smiled at the absurdity of not liking a girl who had suddenly revealed this facet of her nature to him.

"I'm not at all glamorous," said Susan, her pretty little hand resting on her flat tummy.

"That's okay. I'm not as vapid as I look," he cheerfully informed her, thinking what a lovely voice she had and trying to connect it with girls he knew.

"I'm 5'8" and a little bit plump," she reported tentatively, as though it were very important to her to be honest about this. "About a size eleven," she added emphatically.

"What color hair?" he asked, smiling at the thought of an ample bottom.

"Dark brown, short and fairly straight," she replied, stretching a hank of her own medium ash blonde hair out to the full extension of her arm. "And I wear glasses."

"When can we meet, Susan?" Marcus was delighted; he had always loved voluptuous brunettes.

"Are you going to be around tomorrow afternoon?"

"Do we have to wait that long?"

"I haven't decided whether I want to reveal myself to you yet, but if you come to Taylor tomorrow afternoon, I'll probably be there."

Then Susan hung up. The phone rang immediately, but Susan merely smiled and turned the ringer down.

Marcus was not as amused. "You'll reveal yourself to me all right," he promised the receiver with determination.

The next afternoon Marcus entered the Taylor Hall Art gallery at about one and stayed till three, walking around and examining every women who entered, student, faculty and visiting alumni alike. One or two tall, voluptuous, dark haired women came under his intense scrutiny, and he approached them both to ask whether their names were Susan, which thankfully, neither were. Susan, who hadn't counted on him making this direct an approach, sat calmly sketching a Rodin sculpture in charcoals, while her tummy did flips every time he engaged a different large brunette in conversation. What if one of them was indeed named Susan and putting name and demeanor together he suddenly began to scold her? She, the real Susan would have to step in and make her identity known to him on the spot. Still, it made her smile, and she considered it very much to his credit that he was ready to pursue a plump girl with such ardor.

Because he walked around the gallery so many times, he eventually noticed Susan sketching and they exchanged the usual bland, noncommittal smiles reserved for classmates noticed across a lecture hall or in Susan's case, on set crew. Immediately upon noticing Susan, something began to nag at Marcus, but he then saw one of the tall, dark haired girls he suspected of being his correspondent, and in pursuit of her, he forgot about the nagging sensation until much later in the evening.

Susan decided to stay as long as Marcus did in the gallery and completed many quick sketches as she sat there and covertly watched him, though it was almost impossible not to smile when he began to follow one or another big brunette around.

When Marcus finally departed, he looked annoyed, convinced that he had been stood up.

Susan went out that night with her girl gang to the local bar two blocks off the campus and decided to seriously drink. She felt vaguely uneasy about what she had done that afternoon and wanted to put it out of her mind.

After downing half a White Lightning, she became aware of Marcus Gower drinking with some other kids from the drama department in a nearby booth. She told her friends about the events of the afternoon and they all began to goad her into going over to Marcus' table and making a full confession. Susan finished her drink, every gulp of which made her wince, as it included a dollop of every white liquor in the house. Then she stood up on wobbly knees and went over to his booth.

Susan had only been drunk once before, the night that she and Dot got Anthony Newton to take them to his suite at The Copley Plaza and play with them both. This time, however, it was much worse. Her knees were weak and the room was all but spinning, yet somehow she was able to say hello to him in a shy, yet slightly provocative way, which immediately caused him to make room for her beside him in the booth.

"Hi," he said, with the crisp articulation of a sober individual, "It's Susan Ross, isn't it?" He suddenly pulled her name out of a corner of his mind. He'd been introduced to her at least once during a rehearsal and had an excellent memory for names.

"May I sit down?" she asked carefully.

"Please do," he said, happy to entertain such a pretty girl.

"So," she got right to the point, because she was too drunk to focus on anything else. "What did you think of the etchings at Taylor today?"

This remark was innocuous enough. Marcus remembered seeing her sketching that afternoon in the gallery. He looked at her. In fact she had been there the entire time, now that he thought of it. Her name was Susan. And her voice was the same as the girl on the phone.

"I didn't notice the etchings," he said, sternly folding his arms. "I was too busy getting stood up!"

"You didn't get stood up," she returned. "I was there the entire time."

"You sat there and let me go up to total strangers and make an idiot of myself asking them if their name was Susan."

Susan laughed gleefully at the recollection. Because she was drunk, she laughed until her eyes streamed. Marcus, inwardly delighted, regarded her with a sober eye. Finally he said, "I think you've been very naughty."

Susan looked at him with wide eyes.

"I think you'd better come back to my room so we can deal with this right now," he told her firmly, leaving money on the table for his drink and hustling her out of the booth and out of the bar. As Susan's girl friends saw her leave with Marcus they set up a raucous cheer.

Out in the air Susan almost got sick, but as soon as they began to walk she began to feel better. It was very cold so they walked fast, she pulling her leather bomber jacket tightly around her.

"Why did you deliberately mislead me?" he asked her.

"I don't know."

"You deserve a good spanking for doing that," he told her.

Susan didn't dispute this but merely walked along in the moonlight, crunching snow under her soles. Marcus lived in one of the tower rooms of Jewett, eight stories up. Susan's heart was beating so loudly that she seemed to hear it in the elevator.

Marcus had a corner room, with windows on two sides of the building, overlooking the lush, timber cloaked campus, which was now powdered with snow. Up here it was like an aerie. Marcus lit several tall blue candles and drew her over to the bed where he made her sit next to him. But she fell back on the bed when the room began to spin. He helped her out of her jacket, after which she immediately jumped up, stumbled to the door and out to the corridor, which she trundled down with leaden little feet until she came to a bathroom. Without stopping to check whether it was designated for boys or girls she entered this immaculate bastion of ancient blue and white porcelain tile, stumbled past a row of claw footed tubs and sinks dating back to the twenties and immediately locked herself in one of the stalls at the end of the long, narrow room.

Susan could never remember being so sick or feeling so wretched. The worst part was Marcus gently knocking on the door to ask if she needed any help.

"Go away," she whispered weakly, leaning against the wall and clutching her stomach.

"Okay, but I'll be out here if you need me."

He was waiting to grab her as soon as she came out, having washed her face and regained some of her equilibrium.

"I need my jacket," she murmured, walking down the corridor in the wrong direction. He caught her and led her back to his room.

"Are you okay?"

"No," she fell on his bed clutching her head, which was throbbing dreadfully. "Jacket," she repeated.

"You're not going out in the cold again. Just relax and let me get your clothes off," he told her authoritatively.

"No," she pushed his hand away and jumped up, but immediately fell back down. "I have to go. Don't feel well."

"I'll take care of you until you feel better," he said firmly, unlacing her tiny boots and pulling them off, then unzipping her jeans and pulling them off, then unbuttoning the top of her shirt and pulling it off. When she was down to her daintiest white eyelet combination and sox, he pulled back the coverlet and made her get into his bed, which she liked the boyish smell of, even as sick as she was. Then he sat by her side on the edge of the bed and held her hand until her eyes closed and she fell into a light sleep.

Marcus took his Goldoni script and went down to one of the parlors to study his part for an hour before turning in. But when he got back to his room, Susan was gone. She had awoke with a start some twenty minutes after drifting off, found herself alone, hurriedly dressed with stiff fingers, and fled the room. She didn't even wait for the elevator, but ran down the eight flights of stairs to the lobby and burst out into the biting night air again to escape the scene of her humiliation and make her way quickly back to her dorm.

Marcus was very disappointed to find her gone. He'd looked forward to feeling that warm, perfect little body against his that night. What an elusive little bad girl she was!

Susan awoke at ten the next morning feeling hungry and almost normal. But when she remembered what had happened the previous night she pulled the blanket back up over her head.

Surrounding herself with jocular girl buddies she went to the dining hall at noon to partake of the grand buffet luncheon which made Sundays so enjoyable. But Susan did not respond to her friends' raillery. She mused instead on the manner in which she had bungled her evening with Marcus. It was amazing to Susan that she had managed to gracefully play with five sophisticated older men, including her incomparable lover, the composer Anthony Newton, with less trouble than she was having with one fresh, wiry boy. She wondered why she had not taken a more direct approach, as she had so successfully done in the past, with Hugo, Sherman, William, and most recently, Michael. Why did Marcus make her feel so shy? And why did the thought of him laying hands on her fill her with such confusion?

"How are you this morning, young lady?" a voice at her shoulder said. Susan turned to look into Marcus' blue eyes. He had slid into a vacant seat beside her.

"I'm fine, thank you," she couldn't meet his eyes after the initial shock of recognition.

"I'm anxious to see you alone, Susan," he said. "We have a lot of things to discuss."

"I have to work all day," she replied.

"Then tell me when I can see you."

"I have a paper due on Tuesday. I have to work all night too."

"I have a lot of work to do myself but I can make the time to see you. How about it, Susan? You owe me that much for all the inconvenience you put me to yesterday afternoon," he said in a more serious tone, realizing that charm alone wasn't enough to force this young lady to behave in a civilized manner.

"I made a mistake. I apologize," she said.

"You didn't make a mistake when you contacted me."

"Look, don't you understand that I'm mortified?"

"I'm not surprised," he said, "You've behaved very badly."

"I'm very sorry," she explained, pushing away her tray. "I never should have approached you in the first place." She was still having difficulty in meeting his eyes, which were mostly kind and only mildly confident.

"But you did, and now it's time to follow through."

"What if I changed my mind?"

Marcus bristled. "It's too late to change your mind. What's your room number?"

"Main, 432."

"I'll be paying you a visit this afternoon at five."

All of the girls at the table watched him walk away. Susan felt her face radiant with heat.

"Did he look mad to you?" she asked them.

"Smug," observed Virginia.

"He had a rod on," said Debbie.

"I know him, he's a slut," said Judy. "Make him wear a rubber."

"Oh, Susan," said Chris, "are you still playing with boys?"

Susan worked on her Jane Austen paper all afternoon, entranced with the subject matter, until there was a knock at the door of her room at ten to five.

With a pounding heart she let him in and locked the door behind him. As Marcus took in the blue, cream and sand Persian rug, the 21" color monitor on her computer, and the heavy, armless, antique, carved wood, straight back chair which Hugo Sands had sent from his shop in Random Point, he realized that Susan Ross was no scholarship student.

"A young lady with your taste should have better manners," he told her, dropping his overcoat on the bed. She stood with her back pressed against the door, watching him. Marcus didn't hesitate but went directly to the upholstered, straight backed chair and sat down. Then he crooked a finger at her. "Come here, Susan."

"Aren't we going to talk first?"

"No," he said and ended her dilemma by getting up, getting her, bringing her back to the chair and turning her over his knee. This was easily accomplished as she physically yielded the moment his hand closed around her wrist. Because of his general ease around women, Marcus had managed to get a number of girls in this position and actually land swats on their bottoms, but never had one gone over with such compliance before. There was nothing to explain to this one. She was the real thing.

Susan felt a thrill as his left hand curved around her waist to hold her in place. Then the right began to stroke her upturned bottom through her jeans.

"Susan?"

"Yes, Marcus?" she craned her head around to look at him.

"Are you sorry you wrote me that letter?"

"No, not at all," she replied, dropping her head and waiting.

"There was nothing wrong with writing me," he patted her bottom. "However, I can't say the same of our first conversation." Here he began to spank her, giving her ten or twelve hard smacks through her jeans. "Oh!" Susan said or perhaps just caught her breath after each decisive swat. After he stopped, she added, "I'm sorry for lying to you."

"Say you're very sorry," he recommended, administering another six smacks to either cheek. She was aware of a sting and of heat, but her excitement was such that what she felt was not painful. And yet the embarrassment of being spanked like a child of six by a David Lee Roth lookalike was devastating.

"I'm very sorry."

"Your letter was very exciting," he went back to stroking her. "And your voice on the phone so provocative. But then you pulled that prank in Taylor Hall, which quite annoyed me." This remark preceded a spate of much harder spanks, which caused Susan to kick her small feet. Marcus tightened his grip on her slim waist and gave her the sort of spanking he felt she deserved for allowing him to accost total strangers in the art gallery the day before.

"I'm sure you found it very amusing!" he declared during a pause.

"It was funny!" she admitted. "I almost laughed."

"I'll just bet you did," said Marcus, administering another short volley of hard smacks. "Dearest?" he said when Susan caught her breath, "I vote for the jeans coming down now." He helped her back onto her feet, turned her to face him and efficiently unbuckled her belt, unzipped her jeans and pulled them down without a word of protest issuing from Susan's lips, though she rubbed her bottom with a pout.

His deft fingers lightly probed her damp pubic mound through her french cut briefs. She blushed and let him.

After a bit of shoe unlacing and pants pulling, Susan was placed back across his lap in her pretty bra and panty combination.

"To continue with the list of your infamies," he said, acquainting his palm with the seat of her smoky blue silk panties, "we come to your unfortunate overindulgence in spirits last night, which doubtless gave you the Dutch courage you felt you needed to make your true identity known to me."

A vigorous spanking followed, which thoroughly warmed her panties and took Susan's breath away.

"I'm very glad that you finally decided to present yourself to me," he paused to rub her bottom and pull down her panties, revealing her perfect, small, round, jutting, magenta-tinged cheeks. "But I'd like you to admit that you severely curtailed our evening by getting drunk like that."

Marcus administered several dozen more spanks and she took them with a minimum of fuss.

"I'm sorry I ruined everything by getting drunk."

"You didn't ruin it, you merely delayed it."

"I'm surprised you even wanted to see me again after the way I bungled yesterday," she turned to confide.

"Now, Susan, don't be coy. How could I not want to see you?" he massaged her glowing bottom as he held her, ebullient that chance had brought this little princess to him. "As you said in your letter, there aren't many of us around," he turned her around and made her sit on his lap. "Besides the fact that you're adorable in every way and I'm already madly in love with you."

Susan allowed him to kiss her and squeeze her warm bottom.

"I'm also prepared to forgive you and grant full absolution provided you agree to spend the night with me," he added, locking his arms around her waist tightly enough to make her gasp for breath.

"But I have to work on my paper," she protested.

"I mean much later, after you've done all the work you're going to do for the night. I have so much I want to talk to you about."

Naturally, they made love first and talked later. It was the first time Susan had ever stayed up all night. They watched the dawn come up on the catwalk on top of Main. It was very cold that January morning, but Susan and Marcus hardly noticed, because they had so much to tell each other.

By the next day they were boyfriend and girlfriend. They did have sex and frequently. But the primary thrill was spanking. Neither of them could get over the fact that fate had thrown them together like this in a perfect environment.

Both of them agreed that atmosphere and motivation were crucial to any significant scene. Marcus spanked her in every conceivable place and circumstance where he could manage it. He loved to take Susan to the Shakespeare Garden and test her on the names of the flowers. As soon as she drew a blank she'd get a spanking on the spot, turned under his arm. Marcus was well versed in all the sonnets, which included the names of all the flowers in the garden.

He had spent each night with a different girl prior to his first night with Susan, now he wanted no one except her. He tried to keep her with him as much as possible. When he went to work on the paper, he brought her along and made her do caricatures. When he had to study lines, he had her read with him. He read aloud to her and had her read to him. They went to movies together and plays in the city. They went to bars and drank together, but usually only one round. They were eager to get back to one of their rooms to play. There wasn't a perfect place in or around the campus where they hadn't played, including the English class rooms in Avery Hall, where he'd given her her first caning.

Susan's friends in the lesbian girl gang who lived in the townhouses across the road, hardly saw her now. Marsha Hernandez, a tall, butch beauty from the city, and Susan's favorite woman on campus, accused Susan of abandoning her really interesting friends for the white bread pretty boys of the drama department and acting like a heterosexual bimbo.

"You don't understand," Susan explained as they passed a pipe in the living room of the townhouse after the others had gone to sleep or passed out. It was snowing outside and a very old Traffic tape played on the stereo. Candles lit Marsha's clean, chiseled face and caused her black eyes to glitter. "It's a pervert thing," she told Marsha. "Marcus is my soul mate. We're into the same thing."

"What about homeboy in the city?" Marsha referred to Anthony Newton.

"He can't be with me while I'm here."

"I can."

Marsha placed her hand on Susan's blue jeaned knee meaningfully. Susan laughed which made Marsha furious. She got up and paced.

"Look, I can do whatever is necessary to get you off. Why don't you trust me?"

"But I can't do whatever is necessary to get you off."

"You don't have to do jack," said Marsha, "except to let me take you."

"Maybe I'd rather do the taking for a change."

Since Marsha wasn't feeling submissive, she let the matter rest until she could arrange a female-female situation more specifically tailored to Susan's highly esoteric needs.

A few nights after this conversation, Susan and Marcus quarreled for the first time. It was late and they were in bed. It was snowing and the wind battered the panes of glass in the four windows of his room. Marcus had just asked Susan to give him some head and she had impertinently refused.

"I don't do that."

"Really! And why is that?" he bristled at the arrogance of her tone.

"Because it doesn't suit me to," she replied, remembering the horrible night when she had felt obligated to give Master Ollie the blow job. She also recalled the strict lesson Anthony had given her afterward, to teach her not to do things which her instincts recoiled from.

"But it suits me to have you do it," Marcus insisted. "And if you're half as fond of me as you say you are, you should be only too happy to satisfy this simple request."

"It's not a simple request," Susan flared, jumping up in bed. "It's degrading."

"Susan, I don't see how you can say that. Millions do it daily with no loss to pride or dignity," he pointed out patiently. "It is possible that the young lady I thought so adventurous is really a prude?"

"I'm not a prude. I'm just not oral."

"I'd be more than happy to reciprocate. In fact, that was my original intention."

"No thanks," said Susan coolly.

Now Marcus sat up in bed too.

"So you really refuse?"

"Look, you get off just fine with regular sex," she pointed out. "Why ask me to do something I don't really like if you don't really need it?"

"Just because it's an enjoyable thing that lovers do," Marcus felt he was quickly losing ground, especially when Susan got of out bed and began to pull her jeans and boots on.

"Well, I don't enjoy it and I'm not going to pretend that I do," she firmly told him.

"And you're going home? Just because I brought this subject up?" a note of irritation began to creep into his voice.

"I have an 8:30 lecture hall tomorrow morning. It would be better if I left from my dorm," she explained.

Marcus got up and pulled on his jeans, folded his arms across his chest and blocked the door.

"Not so fast. I don't like you leaving like this. Besides, we haven't finished our discussion. Sit down," he pointed to the Winsor chair under the window. Susan sighed and obeyed him.

"You know what I think, Susan?"

"What?"

"I think you're a selfish, spoiled, immature child who doesn't even know what it's like to do something just to please someone else."

"Look, there's lots of things I like that you don't do.

"Like what? Just tell me and I'll be happy to oblige you."

"I've yet to have an orgasm with you," she told him.

"Is this true?"

"You couldn't tell?"

"I wasn't sure."

"But you always have a climax when you fuck me. Don't you?"

"Susan, I'd love to do whatever it takes if you'll only tell me what that is."

"No, it's no good if I tell you. If you're at all into what I'm into, you'll eventually figure it out for yourself."

"Tell me."

"No."

"Susan," he said sternly, and seized her by the wrist only to pull her back to the bed and turn her over his knee.

"No!" she cried in a hushed tone, because it was very late.

"You're a little brat," he told her, warming the seat of her jeans with the palm of his hand. The moment he began to spank her, deep thrills rippled through her groin. He held her fast. "Hold still! Imagine a girl refusing to give her boyfriend a couple of minutes of head!" he intoned with disbelief.

"You let me go," she said, beating his legs with her tiny fists. "You can't bully me into servicing you like a pirate with his wench!"

"I like the metaphor," he told her, smacking her harder through her jeans. "But right now I'm a lot more interested in finding out what secrets you've been keeping from me. What's this mysterious thing you're into?"

"I'm not going to tell you."

"Really? Then I'm going to have to pull your pants down and spank you harder."

"No, Marcus, it's too late. Let me go now and I'll... tell you tomorrow."

He brought his hand to rest on the delectable curve of her bottom.

"Really, Susan," he said with annoyance, reluctantly allowing her to wriggle off his lap and get back on her feet, "I don't know what's made you so contrary tonight but if you're going to be impossible then maybe you'd better go home."

"That was my intention," she infuriated him by coolly replying while sitting on a little stool to lace up her boots. Marcus wished it weren't so late. There was nothing he wanted to do so much now as take Susan out in the woods and wallop the daylights out of her.

"Your insolence is insupportable," he told her severely. He knew many such arcane phrases from reading numerous seventeenth century plays. Susan shrugged and looked like a willful seven year old who had taken offense at her playmate's behavior and decided to home. The pout and ponytail contributed to this illusion.

"I'm going to be a Mistress," she surprised herself by stating.

"Is that so?" Marcus couldn't help but smile at her sudden vehemence. "I had no idea."

"That's right. And Mistresses don't suck boys' pee-pee's."

"Oh, I see."

"I hope you understand," she said condescendingly.

"I understand that you're exasperating the hell out of me."

"Well, I'm going so don't worry," she said, pulling on a wool beret and gloves.

The moment she stepped outside the door of his room she regretted her rash behavior and by the time she got back to her dorm room she was almost in tears. She went to sleep with a heavy weight on her heart, ashamed of the pride she had exhibited to one who was so charmingly modest.

The next morning Susan called her sister Laura.

"Do you give boys head?"

"Well, yes," Laura laughed.

"Do you enjoy it?"

"If the man has a beautiful cock and I like him," Susan's older sister said.

Then Susan called her friend, Marguerite, who was around her sister's age of 30 and even more experienced with men.

"Do you give head, Marguerite?"

"It's been known to happen if I've been sufficiently charmed by the recipient, why do you ask?" Marguerite was greatly surprised at this vanilla sex question coming from the esoteric Susan.

"Oh, because I refused to give my new boyfriend head last night and he became very offended and I'm beginning to wonder whether I was wrong."

"Well, darling, if you don't want to give him head, why don't you thrill him in some other way that you like better, such as letting him take your bottom?" suggested the practical Marguerite.

Susan thought about that all day but finally decided against it. Either a man was into bottoms or he wasn't. The fact that Marcus had never so much as probed her in that area in a month of love making indicated to Susan that he did not deserve to be the administrator of her most powerful fantasies.

Susan went across the road to visit Marsha in the townhouse to ask her opinion of giving head.

Marsha didn't think any boys deserved head.

"Have you ever given head?"

"Oh, frequently."

"To boys?"

"At times."

"But I thought you were a dyke."

"These things happen," she shrugged. "If a boy was really beautiful I sometimes gave in."

Marcus was certainly handsome, in the style of a Calvin Klein model. Susan sighed. Even lesbians seemed to be in favor of Marcus getting head from her.

Just as the sun went down, Susan was trudging out of the library towards the dining hall when she saw Marcus strolling along, deep in lively conversation with a tall, buxom, brilliant brunette named Faye Sanborn, the editor of the school paper. Susan had seen these two together before she and Marcus had ever met and suspected he had some attachment to the confident young woman, who possessed, among her other attributes, a beautifully sculpted, wide, voluptuous mouth. Marcus saw Susan and waved to her with his usual good humor then continued on with Faye. He hadn't called her all day or she him. Susan resolved not to call him till he called her.

Susan might well have rushed back to Marcus on her knees that night, had it not been for an intriguing distraction which had been developing over the last several days in cyberspace. She'd been chatting on her favorite computer bulletin board with a man named Henry Crawford, a dominant, aged 33, who was an avid spanking enthusiast and enema fetishist. He was a high paid tech in an enormous computer company and owned a house in Peekskill, a few miles down the parkway. He described himself as clean cut and conservative in appearance. But Susan hardly cared about that. What fascinated her was his interest in administering enemas to girls. He seemed extremely experienced and owned equipment. Each day they got a little further into the subject. He would describe various procedures and she would become unendurably excited simply reading her E-mail. Sensing her deep and profound interest in the subject, he pressed for a meeting almost immediately, promising to give her the most exciting night of her life.

For several days they went around on the question of what would happen to her if she did agree to visit him. Because she was certain that Henry was going to be a nerd, to whom she could not possibly feel sexually attracted, she had to make it clear that she was not available for sex to him. He replied that he was not expecting sex, simply the exquisite pleasure of humiliating a Vassar girl.

That night she stayed on the board for a couple of hours, exchanging E-mail with Henry and becoming painfully aroused by their discourse. When she finally hung up she had to masturbate. Then she realized that she couldn't continue denying herself this particular adventure when it was occupying her mind so continuously. She fell asleep resolving to call Henry the following day to arrange a meeting.

But the next morning she woke with a guilty start. She remembered how she hadn't done any work the previous evening and had indeed wasted the entire day preoccupied with Marcus in the afternoon and Henry all night. Wondering whether she was becoming a sex addict, she got into a shower and resolved to spend the entire day working on her paper on Pushkin and Turgenev that was due in a couple of days.

After a quick breakfast, at which she was delighted to discover it was Saturday, Susan rushed back to her computer with her notes and novels by her side and opened her file. But as soon as her monitor sprang to color and life she was drawn as one hypnotized to the modem and soon found herself logging into the bulletin board to read Henry's latest message. She stopped herself at the last moment and forced herself to call him instead. He'd given her his number.

"Henry?" her voice was as unsteady as her hand as she lit a cigarette. It was one of several bad habits she'd picked up just in the few months she'd been at school. "This is Susan, from the Board."

"Susan, I'm so glad you called." he had a good voice.

"Look, Henry, I'm ready to agree to your proposal. If I don't I'll never be able to get any work done."

It was settled in a minute. She took down his address and agreed to appear at his house that evening at eight.

After that Susan worked steadily all day, stopping only to eat, stretch her legs and look out the window. Late in the afternoon, Marcus called her to ask her whether she was ready to kiss and make up. She had forgotten about Marcus til that moment, but being a brat she couldn't resist playing the injured party.

"You were with Faye last night, weren't you, Marcus?"

"...Yes," he answered guiltily. "But not the way you think."

"It's okay, Marcus. I don't blame you. You wanted your blow job," she commiserated kindly.

"Listen, you sarcastic little brat --"

"Maybe later. I have to go now."

"Can I see you tonight?"

"No, I have to work."

"For a little while?"

"Maybe much later. After my date."

"What date?"

"Townie with a buzz cut and a pocket protector."

"What do you want with that kind of guy?"

"I can't tell you that. Maybe sometime I will though, when I'm good and drunk."

Susan hung up and went back to work. Ten minutes later Marcus was knocking on her door.

"Okay, what's going on?"

"You fucked someone else last night. I'm free to do the same tonight."

"Is that what you intend to do?"

"No."

"What time will you be back?"

"I'll call you."

"Is this someone in the scene?"

"Would I be wasting my time with anyone who wasn't?"

"I shouldn't let you go," he said firmly.

"I have to get back to work now," she told him.

"I don't like the idea of someone else spanking you," he complained, but meekly went away because she had caught him being a slut and for this he had no excuse.

The fact that he came back to her was cheering. And she appreciated the way he had refrained from bringing up the troublesome subject which had caused this division between them. But now she wanted him to quietly go away so that she could mentally prepare for the evening's adventure alone.

Deciding what to wear was not easy. The weather called for leggings, jeans, cardigans, scarves and down parkas, but the requirements of the evening precluded such practical attire. The object was to achieve maximum accessibility while still keeping on as many articles of clothing as possible. She finally decided on openwork cream crocheted thigh high stockings with rosette sewn stay up tops, a pair of darling little bone Victorian lacing ankle boots, a cream knit lycra camisole and panty combination, lavishly trimmed with flat lace and rosette embroidery, over which she put a fitted camel wool dress with white collar and cuffs. Over this she put the matching camel overcoat and tam. The boots had graceful 3" heels and turned her calves beautifully.

Susan drove over to Peekskill in the jeep which Anthony had given her for Christmas. On the way it began to snow again. Susan could barely contain her excitement at this adventure she had undertaken. She'd decided that unless he was Quasimodo, she was going to stay and let him play with her for a couple of hours. This wasn't the same as going to meet Master Ollie. Henry Crawford wasn't looking for a slave, just a passive girl to examine, cleanse and spank. Repeatedly. That was one of the most arousing aspects of what she was about to experience, that he wasn't satisfied to do it just once. He had a course of therapy planned for her which would take hours to administer.

"If he's awful or I get a vibe, I'm leaving," she told her own reflection in the rear view mirror as she pulled in the gravel driveway of a cream and burgundy Victorian house on a thickly forested street.

She felt her heart pounding violently as she rang the bell and waited for a pleasant but ordinary someone to answer the door. It didn't matter what he looked like, so long as he didn't revolt her. The important part was what he intended to do to her. This man was an enema fetishist. What he was about to do to Susan was his favorite thing. That was crucial to her enjoyment of the situation. It would mean that she could relax and place herself in his hands, trusting him to take care of everything. Plus he owned a double Bardex, which seemed absolutely divine to Susan.

Then the door opened and the floor seemed to turn to sand under Susan's tiny boots. The man regarding her from a height of 6'2" had slicked back, black hair, piercing blue eyes, a Roman coin profile, and the kind of physique it takes a decade to sculpt. When he smiled at her she almost fainted. He took her by the hand and pulled her inside.

"Did I die and go to heaven?" he asked, looking her over.

"You're Henry?" she said.

"Yes. Is that okay?" he locked the door behind her without waiting for an answer and took her coat to hang up.

"But, you never said you were handsome," she protested, allowing him to lead her by the hand into an extremely cozy sitting room, where a fire crackled in a large, marble fronted hearth.

"You never said you were beautiful," he smiled. "But I knew you were."

"Really, Henry, this changes everything," she said, as they sat down on facing wing chairs.

"How about something to drink before we begin. Some fruit juice would be best. And did you fast this afternoon as I recommended?"

"Can I have some coffee?"

"No, juice would be better. You need to be hydrated."

"All right, juice, but it doesn't matter because I've changed my mind completely," she explained, following him into the beautiful wood paneled kitchen to get the juice and then back again.

"Changed your mind? Susan, you'll break my heart now that I've seen you."

They sat down again, he to gaze fondly at her dainty charms and she to blush to the roots as she tried not to meet his curious eyes.

"Look, I was expecting someone plain and ordinary. Someone I could virtually ignore."

"Is that so?" he folded his arms and leveled a glance at her.

"I'm sorry, but I have to tell the truth," she got up and paced. "I was looking forward to meeting a nerd tonight, someone I could feel indifferent to. Someone I could regard as a sort of male nurse. Then I could relax and give in to this perverse desire without worrying about whether I'm attractive to the... administrator."

"You're attractive to the administrator," he assured her.

"I don't think you understand what I'm trying to say."

"Try being more articulate."

"I'd be much too embarrassed to let someone like you do the kind of things me that we've discussed. You're just too good looking. I wanted a robot, someone to whom I couldn't possibly be attracted."

"I see," he looked at her with amusement.

"So you see I have to go?"

"I see I might have to blindfold you to get you to relax," he told her calmly.

Susan looked at him with wide eyes. Perhaps she had fallen asleep in her dorm room and was dreaming this whole encounter. She shook her head and saw that he was still there.

"Now, Susan," he reproved her gently, "you wouldn't want to disappoint me after you told me you were coming to play with me and I've been thinking of nothing else all day?"

"You have?"

"Give me your hand," he told her. She gingerly put her hand out. He pressed it lightly against the front of his trousers, so that she could feel how big and hard the idea of purging her had made his cock. She withdrew her hand quickly, blushing fiercely again.

"You wouldn't like to just pretend we're both normal and skip to the sex right away, would you?" she suggested.

"Now, Susan, I just had you touch me so you could see how turned on I am at the thought of playing with you, but I don't want you to feel that you're compelled to do anything with me tonight beyond submitting to a series of enemas. Okay? Now let's go upstairs."

Henry had arranged his attic as a finished playroom for his hobby. He had a white enamel examining table, upholstered in grey leather, a white wooden cupboard with glass doors which contained his equipment, a real I.V. stand and several white enamel roll away tables. The pitched roof had exposed beams and the floor was of planked oak. Several mirrors hung on the walls opposite the examining table and a grey tweed chair and sofa set completed the room's furnishings. The easy chairs which flanked the couch were armless. There was a grey wooden screen with white paper lining off to one side and she also noticed a door leading to another room, which she suspected was the commode.

"I know you're nervous, but don't worry. I've done this many times before," Henry reassured her. "Now I'd like you to remove your clothes. You can go behind that screen if you like."

Susan went behind the screen and took off her dress. She emerged in the stockings and boots with all her undergarments still in tact. He looked at her and smiled.

"Okay," he said, "we'll go as slowly as you like. Please get up on the table in the all fours position."

Susan found it physically impossible to do anything other than simply stare at the table.

"Susan?"

She hesitated. He then solved the problem by picking her up lightly by the waist and sitting her on the table.

"All fours," he told her firmly. She hesitantly got on her hands and knees. The curve of her bottom was graceful in the clinging lycra briefs. She closed her eyes and felt his broad hand stroke her bottom through her panties.

"You're certainly the prettiest girl I've ever had in this position," he told her, patting her lightly through her panties. "Probably the naughtiest too. Am I right?"

"No doubt," she murmured. So far, so good. Nothing awful had happened yet. He was merely stroking her and admiring her bottom. Then it happened. He pulled her panties down and pushed her camisole up above her waist. She was nude between her waist and stocking tops. And he was dividing her cheeks to examine her.

"Now, Susan," he told her, "you know why you're here so I don't want you to make a fuss while I examine you." He pulled on a pair of latex gloves and lubricated his fingers with KY. Susan held her breath, completely passive now. Once he'd pulled her panties down and exposed her bottom, her resistance dissolved.

But when he began to finger her with the lubricated glove on she lost her poise. His long middle finger snaking in and out of her bottom and the hand he kept firmly pressed against her tummy as he probed her was nearly enough to make her come. She was already so excited simply from having her panties pulled down that this dynamic stimulation was irresistible. She caught herself in the mirror and realized she'd been grinding back against his hand. She looked wanton and seductive. It made her stop and turn around. This made him stop. He removed his finger slowly from her bottom and discarded the gloves.

"You have something to say?" he asked.

"I think we should reevaluate," she told him, breaking the position and sitting down on the table with her legs over the edge and then boldly pulling him towards her by the belt which encircled his trim waist. "I think that you should take me now." She wrapped her arms around his waist and looked up at him. "I'm excited enough without anything else and I feel that you are too."

He hugged her against his lean torso for a few seconds while trying to decide how to handle her.

Finally he said, "No. You're here for a specific reason. You know that." He removed her arms from his waist and placed them back in her lap.

"But I can't let you do all those awful things to me. I'm too attracted to you. How can I let you see me like that and treat me like that when I feel this way? Wouldn't sex alone be enough?"

"Charming," he cupped her peach bosom through the clinging lycra camisole. "Everything about you is adorable," he told her. "But that won't get you out of the treatment you came here to receive."

"It won't?"

"Of course not."

Henry played with Susan for hours, until she was so exhausted that she asked if she might spend the night, whereupon he respectfully placed her in the guest bedroom and left her alone. She slept for an hour then woke and found him setting his playroom to rights. He'd wrapped her in a blue seersucker robe without taking additional liberties.

"Henry? Do you have a girlfriend?"

"Yes, she's out of town this week on a business trip," he admitted, dimming the lights.

"Does she know you're doing this?"

"No. Do you have a boyfriend?"

"I have a couple of people I see," she told him.

"Do they know you're doing this?"

"Not yet, but I intend to tell them all about it."

"It's nice to be able to be open. I'm afraid my significant other is somewhat conventional."

"Does she let you give her enemas?"

"Fortunately, she's into holistic medicine and cleansing so she does utilize my services several times a week, but strictly for maintenance."

"You're saying it doesn't turn her on?"

"Not the way it does you," he smiled.

"Henry, please stop being such a gentleman and take me to your bedroom," Susan said.

After spending the night with Henry, Susan felt even more disenchanted with Marcus and determined to break it off with him.

"He's never even touched my bottom except to spank it!" she said to herself, driving home on the snowy sanded roads. "Marcus was a whim, because I needed someone to play with close by. But now that I know I can reach people like Henry on the network, why should I accept substitutes?"

But when she saw him at rehearsal that evening when she also had set crew, her heart melted. He had such an easy way about him. You simply wanted to smile when he was near. She did smile when she caught his eyes but he returned a haughty stare. This made her tummy grind.

At the first opportunity he walked up to her, took her by the elbow and led her out into the green room, where they could be alone.

"I thought you were coming by late last night," he charged.

"I didn't get home till this morning," she boldly admitted.

"I see," his wide, sensual mouth tightened into a thin line. "Young lady, we have to have a talk."

"Why? It's obvious we're incompatible," she replied, feeling her face grown warm and her heart contract as she saw how these words hurt him.

"Not compatible? You and I? I can't believe I'm hearing this. Just exactly what were you up to last night, Susan Ross?"

"Marcus, this is neither the time nor the place for such discussions."

"Very well, but as soon as we're done here tonight we're going back to my room and have it out," he warned her sternly, then left her there.

Susan sat down in a state of excitement and confusion. Perhaps they weren't as incompatible as she thought. The butterflies didn't lie.

They began to argue as soon as they left Avery Hall.

"Where were you last night?"

"Playing with a man I met on line."

"The computer nerd?"

"His name is Henry. He made me come three times."

This crude statement hit Marcus like a punch in the solar plexus.

"Really! Well, I guess you must have shared some secrets with him that you haven't with me."

"Maybe he just knew the right questions to ask to begin with."

"So what did he do that was different?"

"He played with my bottom," she said, almost indifferently. After what had happened to her the previous night, shame was just a word. "The way you never have or even thought of doing."

This shut Marcus up all the way back to the dorm.

"I don't think I'm going up with you," she said in the lobby. He took her by the hand and pulled her into the elevator.

"How far did you go last night?" he asked her.

"How far did you go with Faye?"

"I kissed her and momentarily groped her bosom," he admitted coolly. "And you?"

"Look, Marcus, you have to understand, Henry is an enema fetishist and I'm anal erotic. We did it all."

"Oh! Is that what your mystery date was about?" Marcus was completely surprised.

"Yes."

"And, do you plan to see him again?"

"No. At least, not for a very long time. He has a girl friend and in any case, the scene was too intense to repeat in the near future."

"But you liked him better than me."

"I didn't say that. He didn't have half your personality or character."

"He was just better in bed," Marcus stated flatly.

"I didn't say that."

They got to his room and he locked the door.

"Sit down," he ordered, pushing her down on the wooden Windsor chair with some emphasis. "I've got quite a bit I want to say to you."

"Such as?"

"Such as I'm very upset with you and your behavior. I thought you were my girlfriend. Now all of a sudden I'm a Philistine and you're seeking esoteric lovers in cyberspace. You think I don't have the imagination to accommodate to your fantasies?"

"I didn't say that."

"You didn't even give me a chance to try. I think that you owe me an apology for that."

"I'm sorry."

"Why didn't you talk to me about this stuff before?"

"It's embarrassing."

"You had no problem bringing up spanking to me when we were total strangers."

"Spanking alone is innocuous."

"Not the kind you're about to get from me," he promised, going into the walk-in closet in search of the new razor strop he'd bought at Caswell Massey in New York the previous weekend.

"Now, are you my girlfriend, or not?" he snapped the strap between his hands as she regarded him with wide eyes.

"What if I say yes?" she asked.

"Then you get a strapping for all this nonsense of the past few days."

"And what if I say no?"

"Come over here," he pulled her over to the bed, sat down, held her between his knees, unbuckled her belt, jerked her dark blue jeans down to her knees and bent her over the edge of the bed. Then he picked up the strop and lay it across her blush colored cotton briefs with a resounding smack of leather on round, girlish backside.

"Oh!" she cried, looking back at him with a fluttering tummy and soft, submissive eyes.

"You're not getting out of this," he told her gravely, laying on another stroke that made her cry out and jump as it stung her pantied bottom. "You've been an inconsiderate, selfish, promiscuous little slut!" A hard volley of three followed. "Leading me on with promises of love and romance, then playing fast and loose with my devoted affections."

"But you admitted that you groped Marsha's bosom two nights ago and kissed her too!"

"That was only some light consolation after your insulting rejection of my modest proposal that we engage in oral sex. I never realized what a brat you are until that moment, Susan."

Now Marcus administered a good, solid set of six swats to the seat of her panties before lowering them to reveal the broad, overlapping swatches of dark rose with which the razor strop had already decorated her pristine, peach colored flesh. Each time the strop came down she caught her breath then gasped as it came away. Now that her bottom was bare, she trembled in fear of the strop and his anger.

"I'm sorry, please forgive me," she begged him suddenly as he raised his arm.

"Maybe later, after you've been punished," he told her, strapping her a dozen times on the bare. These were serious strokes, which quickly brought tears to her eyes. However, she swallowed her sobs and he didn't realize she was crying till he'd completed the round.

"You're a disrespectful little girl," he told her, pulling her around to sit up on the bed, because the twelve hard strokes had already begun to raise angry red marks on her small bottom and he felt that this was enough to impress her with his annoyance. Marcus was pierced to the heart when he saw her face was drenched with tears.

"Oh no," he pulled her against him, with the sort of emotionalism she had never encountered before in the scene. "What have I done? I didn't mean to make my little darling cry," he told her, covering her throat with kisses, which was one of the things he did know she loved.

She clung to him and allowed him to lay her back on the bed. When he saw she'd stopped crying he once again assumed a stern demeanor.

"However, your punishment is not yet complete," he informed her, rolling her over on her tummy so that she once again straddled the edge of the bed. "Stay there," he said and went away to get his riding crop. She leaned up on her elbows and watched him return. When he came back he laid the crop on the bed then briskly divested Susan of her shoes, jeans and panties. He arranged her with a pillow under her tummy and her thighs apart. Then he stood up and went behind her with the crop.

"Tell me again about what you got up to last night, Susan," he demanded.

"No," she stubbornly replied.

A sharp tap with the crop across both her bare, tautly spread cheeks felt like a cane stroke and made her cry out.

"I don't blame you for not wanting to repeat the sordid tale of your shameful behavior," Marcus told her, taking her hands and placing them one on each cheek of her bottom. "I want you to keep your bottom spread open for me until I tell you otherwise. Do you understand?"

"Yes, sir," she whispered, complying with his order as her face flushed with embarrassment. Almost immediately the square leather slapper came down on her upturned bottom crack. She sobbed and caught her breath. The little spank stung and felt shockingly intimate.

"I think it's only proper that I punish this perverse little portion of your anatomy for compelling you to do such naughty things," he told her, once again spanking her tiny, pink bottom hole with the slapper on the end of the crop. "Don't you agree with me, Susan?"

"Yes," she hastened to concur, hiding her face in the pillow.

"Am I to assume you received a thorough cleansing yesterday?" he paused to sit beside her and push her hands aside to himself examine her delightful bottom.

"Yes."

"How many times?"

"Once with mineral oil, twice with salt water."

"And what was the method of administration?" he asked, surprising her by his technical interest. While he questioned her he rubbed, squeezed and probed her perfect bottom, which was still stained dark rose from the strop.

"The first one was given with a syringe bulb and was administered while I lay across Henry's lap," Susan revealed. "The second was given with a regular bag and nozzle, with me on all fours. The third was a larger, retention enema, using a double Bardex, with me on the table in the knees to chest position with my head lower than my bottom."

"This Henry seems a thoughtful fellow. After all the trouble he's gone to, it would be a crime not to take your bottom."

"No!" Susan cried.

"Why not? Don't tell me Henry's done it first and made you sore."

"No, but, you're too big."

"Nonsense."

"I can't."

"You'll do as you're told," he deliberately put her hands back on her bottom. "Spread you bottom for me again, Susan. Now."

"But --"

"Don't argue, you're getting the cropping you deserve," he told her, beginning with the slapper on her bottom-hole again. She whimpered each time he spanked her like this, more excited than hurt by the strict attention. "Get your bottom up," he advised her coolly. "Henry only did half the job last night. The other half consists of punishing you where you'll feel it the most." Six more swats of the square leather slapper followed as he carefully aimed to sting her anus. Then he lay the crop aside and took her hands away.

"Stay in position," he told her firmly, giving her one robust smack on each cheek. "Keep your thighs apart and your bottom up and wait for me."

Marcus was only a moment getting a proper lubricant and divesting himself of all apparel.

"So you had to share your secrets with a stranger, did you?" Marcus wound one hand in her long hair and carefully raised her head without hurting her.

"You didn't seem interested," she murmured.

"Still insolent?" he seemed amazed and let her hair go.

"No!"

"Susan, lower your head and elevate your bottom," he told her, gently bowing her head and pulling her up by the hips. "This is the only way to control you, I know that now," he reported soberly, lubricating her bottom-hole and the shaft of his penis with Astroglide. "This is the best sort of discipline for a brat like you. A good, sound thrashing and sodomizing."

Marcus took her bottom gently but without hesitation, forcing his cock into her tight, throbbing glove inch by inch. "Take it, young lady," he said, spreading her with his hands and firmly slapping her bottom to stimulate and relax her. She sobbed as he plunged in to the hilt and begin to slowly fuck her anally. "Do you understand that that you're being punished for being a capricious little slut?"

"Yes," she found nothing inaccurate in the epithet.

"You need to have your bottom stringently disciplined. Fortunately, I care enough about you to do it. But please be aware that the days of innocent pants warmings in the woods are over. From now you get spanked for real whenever we play. And that means a proper punishment plug in your bottom for every chastisement."

The sensations produced by being sodomized and verbally humiliated simultaneously triggered a shattering climax, which Susan thrilled to for several moments while impaled on Marcus' cock. There was no mistaking the throbbing of her bottom-hole as the orgasm rippled through her and Marcus inwardly rejoiced in his triumph, ejaculating copiously deep inside her core.

"I guess you aren't as vanilla as I thought," Susan said a little later, as she lay locked in his arms with the moonlight coming in the window.

"Vanilla indeed. If I weren't so utterly spent and exhausted I'd thrash you all over again for that," he warned her.

"Marcus?"

"Yes, horror-girl?"

"I'll give you head next time."

"Don't do me any favors."

"No, really. I want to be less selfish."

"Why?"

"Because you deserve an adoring lover."

"I liked the way you behaved just now, taking it in the bottom like the naughty little girl that you are. However, if I ever find out that you've so much as sent this so-called Henry a piece of E-mail again, I will bend you over your little school desk and give you twelve of the best with the English cane that you will never forget!"

Susan felt a tickle in her tummy at these words but retorted saucily, "I'll do exactly as I like, with whomever I choose!"

Marcus sat up.

"You'll do as I say!" he told her, pulling her across his lap and spanking her soundly. "And I say you're going to spend the rest of the semester studying hard and behaving yourself," he paused to stroke and kiss her smooth bottom. Susan didn't argue anymore and soon feel asleep in his comfortable embrace.

Marcus punished Susan every day for a week after her adventure with Henry. Her remark about his being vanilla had stung him. He, who had played doctor from early childhood with any little girl who would let him pull her frilly panties down!

When he showed up in her room and informed her it was time for her punishment, she didn't argue. For he was sternly determined to impress her with his fortitude. Almost losing Susan to Henry had startled Marcus into realizing that he was in love.

Susan confided to Marsha one snowy afternoon, as they shared a cigarette walking out of the art studio, that Marcus had become a guilty pleasure. She enjoyed the voluptuous attentions which he had begun to lavish on her, but knew in her heart how angry and hurt he would be if he felt she was merely using him for thrills. Every day she thought she would bring up the subject of Anthony Newton, and every day she resisted the impulse to do so. Marcus felt so contentedly triumphant at vanquishing Henry that she couldn't bear to apprise him of his more powerful rival.

The first time he had noticed the photo of Anthony Newton on Susan's desk he had commented on it and the collection of cassettes and CD's she had of Anthony's.

"You're a big Anthony Newton fan, I see. Me too," he had said at the time. To which she had replied with an elucidating, "Oh, yes, I love Anthony Newton."

And that was the last time she had mentioned her lover of three years to her boyfriend of three weeks. Now that Marcus appeared to be exhibiting classic signs of infatuation, such as leaving bouquets of flowers in front of her door and mailing her sailor dresses and white frilled panties, Susan knew that she had to tell Marcus something of her situation and she knew it would not be taken well.

"You need a distraction. And I think I know the perfect one," Marsha told Susan, leading her to the Retreat where they got coffee to go with their cigarettes.

Marsha told Susan about a girl she had recently met at a lesbian consciousness raising group on campus, who she suspected was into exactly what Susan was into. This junior, whose name was Diana Stratton, was a spoiled, wild, rich girl from New York who had allowed Marsha to take her back to the townhouse after the meeting and finger-bang her long into the night.

Marsha had told Diana about Susan, how she was into corporal punishment and how she played as often as possible. After which Diana had all but ordered Marsha to bring Susan to her.

That night they visited Diana's room in one of the towers of Joscelyn, which appeared to have been decorated by a Victorian nabob. A Persian carpet, velvet draperies, and exotic incense burners enhanced the atmosphere of the room, in which Diana was reposing when they arrived, curled up on a brocade recamier, with a book of Baudelaire on her lap.

She was an extremely beautiful young lady, 20 years old, peach complexion, about Susan's height and weight, with straight, shiny, light brown hair, chin length, with bangs. She was dressed 50's retro, in a beige cashmere shell and cardigan, a straight, heather brown tweed skirt, oatmeal wool stockings and Italian loafers. Pearls adorned her ears and throat and a charm bracelet circled her wrist. Diana cared about her clothes and the impression she made.

Diana Stratton appraised Susan with clear blue eyes that missed no detail of her visitor's outfit, which that evening consisted of black pegged jeans, small black lacing work boots with rolled sox, and a thin, grey wool shirt over a fine, cream wool thermal top, with a broad black leather belt emphasizing the inward curve of her waist. Her medium ash blonde hair, thick and wavy, was very long by now and Susan wore it in a high pony tail tied with a black grosgrain ribbon. It would have seemed more butch to wear her shirt out, but the way Diana's eyes riveted to her tiny waist made Susan realize she had made the right choice. In fact, their hostess, as she offered them Belgian chocolates, could not take her eyes off Susan's torso, which reminded her of the statue of Venus in the Metropolitan Museum.

"We're the same size," Diana couldn't help pointing out. "You have to let me dress you up and take you out."

"Why don't we just stay in and Marsha and I will undress you?" Susan boldly suggested. Marsha laughed out loud.

"Ha!" intoned Diana haughtily. "Why me? You're the one who's so submissive."

"Really? I heard you were."

"Perhaps I am, but not to straight girls."

"What does it matter if I'm straight, bi or a dyke? You won't know the difference with your head buried in a pillow," Susan pointed out. Diana stared at her and blushed.

"What a charming way of putting it," said Diana, bringing out the best pot that money could buy. As the girls smoked, Diana baited Susan.

"It's hard to believe you've ever dominated anyone, Heather."

"It's Susan," Susan replied coolly and looked at her in such a way that Diana blushed. "But just to satisfy your impertinent curiosity, it's never been a girl, only men at The Vault."

"You've been to The Vault?" Diana's eyes sparkled.

"Many times."

"I've wanted to go there for ever, but I never had anyone to go with," admitted Diana. "Will you take me next time you go?"

"Sure. Any weekend you like."

"So, what are you? A wanna-be lesbian who doesn't eat pussy, or what?"

"Hey," Marsha admonished Diana, "Susan was nice enough to visit you, don't insult her."

Diana looked down at her shoes.

"I'm sorry, Mistress Susan," she peeked at Susan from under her lashes, declaring herself, in these four simple words, available and tractable.

"I forgive you but don't simper," said Susan coolly, strolling about the room to examine Diana's taste in Venetian masks, mirrored dressing cases and many other rare objects.

"Surely there must be a few instruments of correction secreted in this chamber," Susan mused.

"Why, you aren't going to punish me?" Diana could barely keep from smiling. "Not the two of you..."

"Be quiet, slut," Marsha advised. "We'll do as we like with you."

"Found a riding crop!" said Susan, emerging from a corner of the room with a handsome, black crop.

"You wouldn't use that on me!" Diana pretended fear. Susan merely looked at her. Diana subsided.

"I'm going to beat that affected manner out of you," Susan advised her coolly. Diana flushed with pleasure, though she meekly lowered her eyes. Susan took Marsha aside for a conference.

After deciding what to do with her, the two girls approached Diana and put her on the bed on her back. Marsha got her arms above her head and pinned her wrists together to the pillows. Susan separated and knelt between Diana's legs.

"Now behave while we have our way with you," Susan directed, placing each of her hands firmly on Diana's pert bosom through the sweater and shell and squeezing her breasts gently through the cashmere. Diana moaned and her pretty, full red lips parted. Susan lowered her lips to the prone girl's and kissed her new submissive on the mouth. Diana had drunk nothing but milk that night and her mouth tasted sweet. Susan forced her tongue into her new friend's mouth and dominated Diana with their first kiss, then she pulled away. Diana was breathing hard and her eyes were sparkling.

"I hope this is the last time I'll have to answer impertinent questions about my orientation," Susan told Diana, pulling up the brunette's top to expose her perfect, small, round breasts, which were displayed enchantingly in a silk and lace front closing underwire décolleté bra. "Look, Marsha, she wears front closing bras, in order to be accessible to us," Susan remarked. Marsha couldn't keep a smile off her face regarding her two pretty playmates, so comfortably sporting in this manner, but she forced herself to seriously suggest that Susan expose Diana's breasts at once. Susan unhooked the front clasp and pulled the bra open to reveal one of the loveliest, small sized bosoms she had ever seen, with plump, luscious contours and small, saucy, round, rose nipples, now fully erect. Susan squeezed Diana's breasts firmly then pinched the nipples gently. Diana groaned and arched up. Marsha advised Susan to pinch Diana's nipples harder, even put nipple clamps on them, but none of them had any.

"We'll buy some nipple clamps at The Pleasure Chest when we take our slave down to the city to visit the Vault," Susan suggested, lowering her lips to Diana's breasts, to lightly take her nipples between her teeth. Diana purred at this attention. Susan pulled back.

"Breast punishment, I'm told, may be very effective with a certain type of submissive," said Susan, taking careful aim and then slapping Diana's small but full, deep breasts very lightly. This ministration caused the sleek brunette to pant with excitement. This was much more potent a tool for controlling the sensual girl than kisses and bites.

Then Susan pushed Diana's skirt up to her waist, revealing a pair of full, silk briefs, lavished with lace, in a pale sand color, to match the brassiere. Susan placed her palm against Diana's Venus mound through the crotch of the panties. Marsha shifted her hold on Diana, letting go of her arms and moving down to enclose her now bare bosom in her two strong hands and hold her in place. Marsha also lowered her mouth to Diana's and explored it with her tongue.

"Ordinarily, I might take the time to finger-bang you through your panties for a while," Susan told Diana, squeezing her crotch through the panties as the panties became damp from Diana's excitement, "but I can't wait any longer to punish you for that Heather remark. So roll over!"

"Roll over? But why? No!" Marsha and Susan rolled Diana over and pressed her down on her tummy.

"Beautiful hair," Susan commented, running her fingers through Diana's straight, thick, shiny brown hair.

"She's such a bad girl," said Marsha, straddling Diana's back facing her bottom and slowly pulling up the tweed skirt. The panties were even more lavish on the backside and the treasure they clove to exquisite. It wasn't just the beauty and symmetry of Diana's round, jutting cheeks which took Susan's breath away. Her shapely legs, so smooth above the tops of the oatmeal stockings, so slim as they tapered to her knees, so voluptuous as the well developed muscles of her calves tautened under Susan's caresses, were equally divine.

"You can see how badly she needs someone to pay attention to her bottom," Susan remarked, as she kneaded Diana's firm, creamy buttocks through the expensive French knickers. Diana sighed in assent and even said, "Thank you for paying attention to my bottom, Mistress."

Susan smacked her sharply.

"Did I ask you to speak?"

"No, ma'am," Diana replied, concealing a smile in the pillows as she ground her tingling pussy against the rich counterpane. Marsha enclosed Diana's tiny waist between her hands to keep her in place as Susan slowly lowered her panties.

After baring her bottom, Susan and Marsha simply stared for several seconds in silent appreciation. They looked at each other and smiled.

"It's as smooth as a baby's bottom," said Marsha, venturing to caress one cheek.

"I can't resist feeling how smooth it is," said Susan, leaning down to rub her face against her new friend's flawless skin, which was extremely beautiful and peach toned. Diana ground against the bed until Susan smacked her.

"Lie still. We aren't done examining you yet," she warned Diana. Marsha took this cue and placing one hand on each satiny cheek, divided the pampered bottom and revealed the delicate rose-hued portal in between to Susan's fascinated gaze. "Keep her bottom spread like that," Susan directed, firmly pulling Diana up by the hips in order to thrust a pillow under her tummy and elevate both her bottom-hole and labia. Diana uttered an inarticulate noise which betrayed her acute excitement at this operation, convincing Susan of her anal orientation.

Remembering how Marcus had used the crop on her bottom-hole in the not too distant past, Susan began to use the square leather spanker at the end of the crop to sting Diana's anus. This particular attention to her bottom electrified Diana, who couldn't help but begin to grind against the pillow again. Susan lay the crop aside. "What did I tell you?"

"I'm sorry!" Diana whimpered.

"Don't you deserve a good whipping?"

"Yes, Ma'am!"

"Then hold still."

"I will," Diana promised, casting them both a lingering look over one shoulder.

"Put your head down and be quiet," Susan advised her and delicately began to separate the petals of Diana's labia with her fingers.

"Ooooh!" said Diana as Susan carefully inserted one middle finger into her new submissive's pussy, which had become extremely wet over the last several minutes. Meanwhile Marsha reached down into a drawer below the bed for the tube of KY which she remembered from a previous visit. Marsha, still straddling Diana's back, lubricated her long middle finger and slowly began to insert it into Diana's split bottom-hole. Diana squirmed and panted. Susan spanked her with her hand until she settled down then went back to fingering her pussy. Now Marsha finger-fucked Diana with one hand and spanked her with the other while Susan did the same to her pussy.

"Now press your exposed bosom against the pillow," Susan told Diana, adding two more fingers to her sopping wet pussy. "And think about how it's going to feel the first time I shove a thick, rubber dildo into your bottom before paddling you over my knee."

Diana succumbed at this idyllic image and gave herself up to a heavy climax under the masturbation and light discipline. She turned around, still shuddering, and now in love with Susan.

The next morning Susan received a lavish bouquet of white orchids with a note that read, "Who ever heard of a blonde dominating a brunette. I adore you and I am your slave. Diana."

Susan had gone to sleep musing on the ravishing buttocks and legs of her new friend. She had never consciously fantasized about another girl before, but her experience in Diana's room had left a rapturous impression on her. She was amazed to find herself thinking about another girl's body, but realized that this sophisticated young lady had finally aroused the predator in her. So this was how men felt when they looked at her. The combination of Diana's accessibility, sexual submissiveness and sheer prettiness had been more than enough to prod Susan into turning top.

Susan began spending a small amount of time with Diana every day, studying her new friend and her needs. Susan discovered that Diana's nature made her accessible to anyone who simultaneously pleased and took a dominant tone with her. Although she had recently sworn off boys as sexual partners in favor of the females she preferred, she had no objection to receiving spankings and whippings from intelligent men and would also allow her bottom to be taken with fingers and toys. To Susan this seemed more than generous to the male sex, though she fully understood that Diana's desire to be the object of discipline outstripped every other sexual inclination she possessed at this point in her life. They discussed all of this late one night, over cigarettes and coffee in the half darkened gold parlor.

"Of all the girls who ever sat on this settee, how many do you think wanted their lovers to dominate them?" Diana mused, regarding the heavily brocaded Victorian sofa upon which her graceful form now curled.

Susan merely smiled because the question had no answer. The sofa had been part of the room's furnishings for a hundred and thirty years and thousands of young ladies had sipped their demitasse while perched upon it, some in tightly lacing corsets, some in bobby sox.

"Now remember, Diana, we're going down to New York this weekend and we're going to play at The Vault."

"Shall we stay at my house or yours?"

"We'll stay with my lover and have his chauffeur drive us to and from The Vault on Friday night in the Bentley."

Diana much preferred this plan to staying on Park Ave.

"But what's your lover like? Some boring, thirty-five year old stock broker who looks like Ralph Bellamy?"

"Oh no, Anthony's completely loveable. More like the young Don Ameche."

"Show me his picture," said Diana. So Susan took her up to her room and handed her the framed eight by ten black and white glossy of Anthony which Diana had seen any number of times already.

"Anthony Newton is your boyfriend?" Diana gazed at the portrait with the admiration of one who is unabashedly impressed with name, rank and position.

"He has been for some time. "

"How delightful," Diana said.

"Aren't you curious about how I came to be his girlfriend?"

"I assume you moved in the same circles?"

"Don't be ridiculous. What do I have in common with a Broadway composer who's twenty years older than me?"

"You lived in the same apartment building and met in the elevator, where he was instantly smitten with your beauty and then proceeded to woo you with bon bons and soft toys from FAO Schwartz?"

"No, and couldn't you come up with anything better than that? Do I seem insipid to you?" Susan leaned forward and pinched Diana's earlobe between two fingers. Diana caught her breath and blushed.

"I'm sorry!"

"Anthony and I were introduced through a connection in the scene."

"And am I to understand that this gentleman is the one who spanks my mistress?" Diana regarded the photo with as an honored relic.

"It has been known to happen."

Diana stared at the photo.

"He is extremely handsome," said Diana. "Will he be at home when we arrive?"

"Possibly. Would you like to meet him?"

"Of course I would. How could you doubt it? I've seen all of his musicals three times. I'd want to meet him even if it weren't for the scene. Does he spank hard?"

"Sometimes. Why?"

"I want to play with him."

"Play with my lover?" Susan pretended to be irritated.

"Only if you're there, Mistress!"

"I'll see what I can do," Susan promised.

But when they were driving into the city on Friday afternoon, Susan brought up their favorite subject with some trepidation.

"Diana, are you sure you want to reveal this side of yourself to Anthony? I mean, he's a perfect gentleman, of course, but if you provoke him, you might not be happy with the results."

"Oh, Susan, I fantasize about being spanked by older men all the time. I've even sent anonymous slave letters to Mr. Gregg in the Russian department."

"So, you really want me to be frank with Anthony about what a slut you are?"

"Oh, please! That will save me the embarrassment of having to be forward."

Susan wanted to know whether Diana would play with Marcus too.

"Well," Diana said, "he's terribly handsome, but can we count on him to punish me severely?"

Susan smiled at her new friend.

"He probably should, considering you're stealing my heart away from him," Susan informed Diana.

"Oh, he doesn't have to know that."

"For a lesbian you're kind of soft and fuzzy on boys, why is that?"

"Not all boys," Diana quickly pointed out, "Just the ones who are as perverse as me. If a male longs to worship my perfect bottom, why should I deny myself this homage?"

Diana cuddled against Susan as they barreled down the Taconic Parkway in the twilight of a frosty February afternoon. "I'm so glad I met you," confided Diana. "With you, all my dreams can come true."

About the Author

In Random Point, everything is linked to spanking and this is true for the author of the Shadow Lane novels as well. Eve Howard has been writing and producing spanking erotica since the 1980's, when she began freelancing for one of California's largest fetish magazine publishers. While editing *Spank Hard* magazine (as Lizzie Bennett) in 1985, she was discovered by the video producer Nu-West and offered a chance to perform in spanking videos. In 1986 she published the first Shadow Lane story and the following year formed the video production company Shadow Lane with her partner Tony Elka. The Shadow Lane novel series, originally published by Eve in serial form in her magazine *Stand Corrected*, was brought out in paperback volumes by Blue Moon books beginning in 1992. There are nine titles in the Shadow Lane series and Eve is currently working on Volume 10.

Since 1988, Eve has written, directed and produced over 140 spanking videos, the vast majority featuring the same male-spanks-female dynamic portrayed in her novels. Female-friendly and designed to make people feel good, rather than guilty, about being into spanking, Eve suggests an irreverent alternative to the all or nothing B&D subculture portrayed in such beloved classics as *The Story of O.* Many spanking fans have discovered the real life spanking scene by following the same patterns of social networking as described in the Shadow Lane novels. And for almost twenty years, Eve's company Shadow Lane has been one of the primary social organs of the real life spanking scene. She lives with her husband Tony and three cats in Las Vegas.

Reader Reviews about the Shadow Lane Series

"I've become addicted to the "Random Point" series so much that I can't wait until the next chapter. I've ordered the first two Shadow Lane volumes and have re-read them over and over. I never tire of them. Eve is the only person I know who can make an enema sexy."

"I discovered Shadow Lane about a month ago via AOL. Prior to that time I thought I could write excellent spanking erotica. Then I ordered, "The Problem with Laura." This is just a note to commend Eve Howard's spectacular talent and to say thanks for an incredible erotic experience."

"I have just completed "Return to Random Point" and decided that I had to write about how much I enjoyed it. I have not been so aroused since reading my first discipline novel many years ago, about a girl raised in England and "coming of age" as I believe they put it. More recently I have enjoyed reading Grant Andrews' My Darling Dominatrix and Ann Rice's "Beauty" series. It seems that women, though, have the right touch when it comes to writing about this subject. Eve, especially, knows how to touch that erotic nerve and bring it to a pure, raw sensuality until one feels that he/she is near bursting with lust."

"I, for one, have always loved (and by loved I mean devoured... breathlessly) Eve Howard's novelettes. To read them… especially when I was just 'coming out'... was to feel completely validated. I truly identified with each and every heroine; the feisty, sassy ones, the shy, demure ultra 'subby' ones... the young ones, and the more mature. I loved the gentle yet firm "taken in hand" nature of the romantic variety of spanking D's that Eve always incorporated into the stories. I loved that the plots were not complicated… but, feasible nonetheless. I loved the depictions of sexual escapades after many of the spanking interludes. I appreciated that the girls were cherished and adored by the affably rogue-ish gents… that the submitting was willing and desired… that it wasn't like 'rape.'

I like the settings... having grown up in New England and living here almost my whole life. I LOVED the idea of the bookstore (which I always find sexy). Then and now. I could cite many passages too, but I fear I've rambled enough. Eve was/is always my favorite spanking author."

www.ingramcontent.com/pod-product-compliance
Lightning Source LLC
LaVergne TN
LVHW090948080826
845145LV00003B/932
* 9 7 8 1 9 2 6 5 8 5 2 9 1 *